Free to Fly

A Novel of Post-Abortion Healing by . . .

Savannah Grace Groden

WestBow
PRESS
A DIVISION OF THOMAS NELSON

Copyright © 2013 Savannah Grace Groden.

All rights reserved. No part of this book may be used or reproduced by any means, graphic, electronic, or mechanical, including photocopying, recording, taping or by any information storage retrieval system without the written permission of the publisher except in the case of brief quotations embodied in critical articles and reviews.

Unless otherwise noted, all Scripture quotations are from the
New King James Version of the Bible.

The story and its characters and entities are fictional. Any likeness to actual persons, either living or dead, is strictly coincidental.

This book is designed to provide information and motivation to our readers. It is sold with the understanding that the publisher is not engaged to render any type of psychological, legal, or any other kind of professional advice. The content of the book is the sole expression and opinion of its author, and not necessarily that of the publisher. No warranties or guarantees are expressed or implied by the publisher's choice to include any of the content in this volume. Neither the publisher nor the individual author(s) shall be liable for any physical, psychological, emotional, financial, or commercial damages, including, but not limited to, special, incidental, consequential or other damages. Our views and rights are the same: You are responsible for your own choices, actions, and results.

References are provided for informational purposes only and do not constitute endorsement of any websites or other sources. Readers should be aware that the websites listed in this book may change.

WestBow Press books may be ordered through booksellers or by contacting:

WestBow Press
A Division of Thomas Nelson
1663 Liberty Drive
Bloomington, IN 47403
www.westbowpress.com
1-(866) 928-1240

Because of the dynamic nature of the Internet, any web addresses or links contained in this book may have changed since publication and may no longer be valid. The views expressed in this work are solely those of the author and do not necessarily reflect the views of the publisher, and the publisher hereby disclaims any responsibility for them.

Any people depicted in stock imagery provided by Thinkstock are models, and such images are being used for illustrative purposes only.

Certain stock imagery © Thinkstock.

ISBN: 978-1-4497-9278-7 (sc)

Library of Congress Control Number: 2013907307

Printed in the United States of America.

WestBow Press rev. date: 5/13/2013

Where can I go from your Spirit?
Or where can I flee from Your presence?
If I ascend into heaven, You are there;
If I make my bed in hell, behold, You are there.
If I take the wings of the morning,
And dwell in the uttermost parts of the sea,
Even there Your hand shall lead me,
And Your right hand shall hold me.
Psalm 139:1-8 NKJV

Chapter One

Killer, that's what she was, according to the billboard at least. As she drove by the fifteen by fifty foot indictment, the horror slowly faded, to be replaced by a deep longing emptiness and latent thread of uncertainty. She had been a Christian long enough to know that God forgives sin. In her heart of hearts, she wondered if maybe this one wasn't just a little too big, even for God.

She continued the drive to her grandparent's house, tires easily eating up Interstate 70 as she continued across Kansas toward the Nebraska state line. It was nearing the end of the wheat harvest, and mile after mile of farmland was giving up its golden crop to combines and farm trucks, destined for someone's loaf of bread or box of cereal. Dust and chaff had colored the sky with an ochre haze that promised fat paychecks for farmers, and resulting revenue for their suppliers, implement dealers, banks and restaurants.

She rolled her window halfway down and blew the city air out of her lungs, drawing in a deep breath of freshly turned soil, green grass and home. She felt something in her ribcage relax. Pushing her straight blonde hair out of her eyes, she wondered how things could have gone so wrong so fast. Feeling the need to stretch her legs and relieve herself, she took the off ramp to Kingdom City, which looked like a carbon copy of the other small towns she had seen along I-70. Several gas stations, the inevitable fast food restaurants, a church, and a shop or two, mixed and matched according to the needs of each community. Grain elevators dotted the distance, and an occasional farmstead, but fields of wheat, now standing empty, surrounded her as she stopped her sports car and shifted it into park.

Grabbing her purse, she headed for the sign that said restrooms, all the while keeping a wary eye for anything that might look even a little bit out of place. Her job as a salesperson for a pharmaceutical company had taken her into many rest stops like this in the last two years, and her cautious nature, continual reminders from her family, and her own terrifying experience had combined to make her keenly aware of her surroundings. She flinched instinctively and drew her hand to her heart, as if the physical touch could drain away the pain that still lodged there. The pain subsided to a dull ache as she finished her business and paid for a fountain soda and cheese curls. This was going to have to be lunch, because she didn't plan on making any more stops until she neared the Kansas/Nebraska line, and whatever awaited her there.

Chapter Two

She continued down I-70, the singing of the wheels and the distance behind her already providing the comfort of anonymity. When her name had been leaked to the local news media, she had come to near celebrity status in the St. Louis area. Never mind that rape victims identities were supposed to be protected. When the fight over a bill aimed at revamping Missouri's antiquated foster care system coincided with the news that the young man who had attacked her was a product of that faulty system, she had unknowingly and without her consent become the poster child for foster care reform. She sighed and tried to leave the past behind. All she could think of was finding the respite of her grandparents' farm in the small town of Purchase, Kansas.

The thing about a small town was everyone knew your business. The beauty of it was they didn't judge you for it. They would sit around at the café and wonder how it happened, but if you were one of theirs, they'd never turn their back on you. Her lip caught between her teeth in thought. At least that's how she remembered it.

A green highway sign indicating her last turn before home flashed by as semi's and bread trucks and families in minivans raced with her toward the border. In a simpler world, she would be getting excited about her escape from the city and her job for six weeks. Today she felt almost like she was being driven.

After the rape, they had said to take some time off to rest and recover, both mentally and physically, and Gleason Pharmaceuticals would be happy to pay for it. The corporate counselor had given her the names of several psychologists, should she feel the need to use one, but Chelsea hadn't felt the nudge to tell a stranger or group of strangers about the experience that had changed her life.

Maybe if she had sought some advice, she thought, her second mistake wouldn't have happened. After that terrible misjudgment, they told her that she could go back to work right away. There would be no after-affects. All it had done was pile crying on top of misery. No one but her best friend knew about the pregnancy and abortion. It wasn't something you told just everybody. Not even Gram.

She loved her grandmother, who had taught her all of the life lessons that had made her successful at college and beyond. Show up on time, do your best, tell the truth. The truth would be a little harder to tell this time, she thought. Enough. She closed the mental door to her past and determined to press on to her new future. One that held the promise of her Father's love and His perfect plan.

It was her grandfather, though, that held a special place in her heart. In fact, she had dreamed about him and her pet rabbit Henry the night before. She must have been about five in the dream and was visiting her grandparents for the summer. She remembered getting up and seeing Henry's snow white fur scattered all over the back yard. She had climbed up into her grandfather's lap and cried her eyes out. She could almost feel the smooth fabric of his worn overalls against her face as she rested her head against his chest and listened to the sound of his heartbeat. They had rocked and rocked and he told her stories.

His stories had both distracted and comforted her, and her tears had faded away with the soft cadence of his voice as he told her stories of life on the Midwestern plains. Even at that age it had made her feel rich. It was her history too.

She continued to follow the white stripes in the middle of the roadway that would lead her home. She forced her hands to relax on the wheel. The past was retreating behind her with every beat of the expansion lines in the old concrete highway. Thump, thump, thump, just like the beating of her grandfather's heart. She smiled at the thought of the old man's face, wheat stalk dangling from the corner of his mouth and clear blue eyes that seemed to know the truth about a thing before anyone ever spoke about it. Her only hope of not being found out was to cover over her secret and bury it deep.

Chelsea drummed her fingers on the steering wheel and tried to second guess the decision she had made. She knew not many would condemn her. She was one of the small percentage of women who had an abortion due to rape or incest. She had always felt sorry for those victims when she heard statistics about abortion. She could never really fathom what might lead a woman to take the life of her child. Now she had joined their ranks. "Killer"—the billboard said in so many words. The shaft of pain she had felt in the days since her choice shot through her heart like a bolt of lightning, searing the frayed edges of the wound and condemning her mind. Yes, the rape had been out of her control. The loss of her child, she told herself, had not.

She pulled off the road, laid her head on the steering wheel, and let the tears come. Why hadn't someone told her? She cried tears of loss and sorrow, both for her past and for her future. Her life had unalterably been changed the day of the rape, and changed again that day at the clinic. Because of the news coverage, everyone in the St. Louis area knew about the rape. Chelsea was going to make sure no one ever knew about the abortion. Too much pain. What she needed was a few weeks to get her act together and all she could think about was going home. Back to Purchase, where the memories were pleasant, and the past would be 700 miles away.

Chelsea gathered the spent tissues and stuffed them in the side pocket of her purse. If only her mind could be cleared that easily. Old thoughts carefully wadded and tucked away, ready to be tossed out when she reached her destination.

Turning on her blinker, Chelsea guided the car back onto the incessant, bleating traffic of I-70. Like sheep without a shepherd, they were all on their way. Some of them just didn't know exactly to whom or where they were headed.

Chapter Three

A dusty white mailbox signaled Chelsea's turn into the long lane leading to the Livingston's farm. The tires crunched on the white gravel driveway as she drove slowly toward the wooden two-story farm house. She looked up to see Grandma Sharon on the front porch, her arms already extended, as if she could draw Chelsea into a hug before she ever got out of her car. Chelsea's eyes closed momentarily and she let out a deep sigh. She heard the wheels of her car thump as she crossed a small bridge over a dry streambed. She felt like those stones in the dry creek bed. She was ready for a shower to wash away the accumulated dust and dirt. She was ready for some rain to wash away her past. She was ready to begin again.

Gram's smile of gentle welcome was balm to Chelsea's soul, and she longed to sink into those arms and have Gram tell her that everything was going to be all right. Chelsea knew deep down in her heart that everything would be all right. One of her favorite verses from the Bible began to run through her mind.

"*Many waters cannot quench love, Nor can floods drown it . . .*"

That scripture was one of the things that had kept her from becoming an emotional blob during the capture and trial of the man who had assaulted her.

Grandpa Pete stood next to Gram by the time Chelsea brought the sports car to a stop. She sat in the car and waited for the cloud of white dust to settle around her. She smiled at the thought of the timelessness of the country around her. She had been fascinated by Grandpa's stories of living on the Midwestern plains. Stories of her great-grandfather's struggle to feed the family during the Dust Bowl, when most of the dirt in Kansas was air-born instead of the firm foundation that every other year had held the crops that sustained them. "You know, Chelsea girl," her grandfather had said, "your great granddaddy said the only thing they had to eat for 'pert near a whole year was jackrabbit. Stewed jackrabbit, baked jackrabbit, fried jackrabbit. Great-grandma said if she never saw another jackrabbit, it would be too soon for her. Grandpa said he was always grateful when he saw a jackrabbit. It was like manna sent from the Lord to feed his hungry family. That Dustbowl 'pert near drove them off this land. I'm a grateful man that it didn't."

She smiled at the memory, opened her car door, gathered her things and headed up the porch steps and into the arms of her grandmother. She lifted up a silent prayer to God, thanking Him for His faithfulness and for bringing her safely back to this place.

Chelsea followed her grandfather and her luggage through the wooden screen door while her grandmother went to put the finishing touches on dinner. The smell of baking bread made her mouth water as she followed Gramps up the stairs and into her old bedroom. It looked the same, except for a pair of new curtains in the window and a colorful new rug on the smooth wooden floor in front of the four poster bed. Her grandfather gave her a gentle hug and retreated down the stairs. Chelsea wanted to plop down on the bed and sleep for a week. Instead, she freshened up in the bathroom next door and went back downstairs. She followed her nose into the kitchen, and saw Gram dishing up dinner, and Grandpa carrying it to the table in the dining room.

"'Bout time you were back at this table," Grandpa said, winking at his favorite granddaughter.

They held hands and said grace, a ritual that had been happening around the table as long as Chelsea could remember. She was overcome with thanksgiving for the two older people who had meant so much to her. They had raised her since she was seven, and her years had been full of love and support and the wisdom that comes with age. The time around the table was full of what had been happening on the farm and in the community of Purchase, and delicious food. By the time they pushed away from the table, she was relaxed but weary. It had been a long drive, and a longer day. When the dinner dishes were cleared, they went back out on the porch. Chelsea sat in the rocking chair, Gram in the swing, and Grandpa stood against a porch post, looking out over the freshly combined fields.

Chelsea noticed the gray paint on the porch floor could use another coat. Maybe she could help Grandpa put a fresh layer on the already thick layers of paint underfoot. It would be fun to spend some time with the older man who had done so much for her. Gram had said that the harvest had taken a lot out of him this year. Chelsea wondered if it hadn't been the worry of the attack and trial that had wearied him, along with the responsibility of harvest time on the farm. She would see what she could do to help around the farm while she was home. Her grandparent's weren't getting any younger.

"The pot roast was delicious, Gram," Chelsea said, smiling at the older woman as she rocked gently, putting her hand on her full stomach. She had indulged a little since it was her first night home. Pot roast with potatoes and carrots, home-made rolls and cherry pie. All the comfort foods Chelsea remembered from her years on the farm.

"Your Grandma can put on a real feed," Grandpa said, chewing on a stem of wheat stubble, staring out into the field in front of the house.

"The potatoes weren't mine this year," Gram said. "With this touch of arthritis and the hours at the food pantry, I just don't have as much time for the garden."

"You do plenty lady," the older man said affectionately. "We've got enough vegetables in the pantry already to last a couple of years." He looked toward Chelsea and made a motion toward his wife. "She's head of the food bank committee this year, and it takes up a lot of her time, but she still manages to keep the cookie jar full for the old man," he said, winking.

Chelsea smiled at their easy banter and enjoyed the breeze. She thought again how blessed she was, having a place like this to come home to. The familiar shaft of pain stole through her heart like a jolt, leaving the edges of the wound frayed. She grabbed the soft rounded arms of the wooden rocker, her pain causing her to tense. The past was behind, she reminded herself. She had come to Purchase to plan a new future. She mentally buried the pain deeper, refusing to let it see the light of day or affect her future.

Free to Fly

They rocked in quiet companionship, listening as the crickets began to chirp and the frogs started their evening chorus of croaks and grunts.

"Are things alright in St. Louis, Chelsea?" Gram asked, not breaking the momentum of the gentle swinging. "We're so thankful you're here, and you know you're welcome to stay as long as you like. Grandpa and I were both sorry we left you in St. Louis by yourself after the trial. We should have stayed."

Chelsea got up and went to sit beside Sharon Livingston in the swing. Laying her head on her grandmother's shoulder, she was about to protest.

Gram laid a hand, wrinkled and tan from years in the sun on Chelsea's arm. "I know you didn't think you needed us, and maybe you didn't, but the hardest thing I've ever done was drive away and leave you in that apartment of yours. We almost turned around about halfway home. You were old enough and smart enough to make your own decisions, but we worried about you."

Chelsea covered her grandmother's hand with hers. "I'm sorry that I caused you to worry. I knew you needed to get back to the farm, you needed to watch the wheat." When the wheat was nodding, they only had a few days to get the combines in the field to guarantee a good harvest. A hard rain or strong wind could cause the grain to shatter, leaving the heads on the ground, unable to be used. Grandpa had the neighbors watching the crop for the days he was gone, and the wheat had been fine, but Chelsea had felt better when they both were back home in Purchase. "I'm fine. You did enough, staying the entire time the trial. You don't know how much it meant to me to have you there." She meant it too. She didn't know what she would have done if she'd had to face the trial alone. Grandma and Grandpa would have never let that happen.

"I'm using the time they suggested I take off because of the attack. I thought the best place to use it was here with you and Grandpa. Surely there's something that needs to be done to keep me busy for a few weeks."

"Oh, I imagine we can find something," Gramps said, winking at Gram.

Chelsea sensed a silent conspiracy. She wondered what they had in mind. Whatever it was, she was ready. She was ready for change. She rocked quietly, enjoying the peace that had enveloped her as she turned up the drive to the farm. Her mind drifted back to the man who had been found guilty after so many weeks in the courtroom. He would be in jail for a very long time, and Chelsea could actually say she felt sorry for him. She had known from the first day of the trial, that God's Word had required her to forgive him. Sitting in the courtroom day after day, hearing the story of the way the young man had been raised had allowed her to do that. She had mentally chosen every day to forgive him, and by the end of the two weeks, her heart had begun to agree with her. She had sat in the courtroom and seen a man who through no fault of his own, had become a victim at the age of seven of a faulty foster care system when he, himself had been a victim of abuse that lasted for years. Where was God when all this was happening to this young man? Chelsea wondered. Maybe no one had ever introduced them. The bitterness had drained away as she became intensely aware of how favored her life had been up to this point. She had grown up surrounded by the knowledge that she was loved, by her friends, family and God. She had never gone hungry, and had always had a real home. This man had never even had a whiff of the kind of life Chelsea had led. Somewhere along day ten, the forgiveness she was choosing in her mind became reality in her heart. Her mind came back to the present as Grandpa interrupted her thoughts, the wheat stalk bobbing up and down as he spoke.

"Actually a few of the neighbors will be combining the Ross's property in the morning. Do you remember me telling you that he had caught his arm in the auger, cleaning the last of his grain from the bins? He's in no shape to bring in the wheat, so we're going to make a day of it at his place tomorrow," Gramps said. "Matter of fact, his boy's home for a few weeks. You remember him? He brings the message occasionally at church services, and works with the youth on special projects. Tall, good looking feller'."

Chelsea thought back to the times she'd visited in the last three years. "I just haven't been home enough to have seen him, I guess," Chelsea said, moving the swing gently with the toe of her shoe as she sat next to her grandmother. She had been too busy with her new career, and had made it home only for a few holiday weekends in the three years she had been gone. She should have done better. She planned to make up for it in the weeks to come.

"Make sure I'm up Gram, and I'll help with the food." Chelsea knew they would be fixing food to take over to the Ross's. There would be a dozen combines and as many grain trucks lining up to consume the heads of wheat that still stood on the twelve hundred acres the Ross's farmed. Pops Ross was a tenant farmer, and only half of the proceeds actually stayed with the Ross's, but it had been a pretty good year, weather-wise, and they should have plenty to pay back their seed loans and have enough to live well until the next harvest. Time ran in Purchase like it did in the Bible-- seedtime to harvest. The hands on the clock may turn, and the moon may move across the sky, but the heartbeat of Kansas was the wheat.

"God's clock," Grandpa used to say, "doesn't run by train schedules and an imaginary line called the Prime Meridian." Chelsea knew that in Kansas, God's clock started with the ground frozen solid, hiding the seed that lay dormant. It lay fallow, gathering nutrients and strength until the length of days and temperature of the soil signaled the tender shoots to break open the topsoil and grow toward the sun.

Chelsea was always amazed that the tender shoots pushed through such amazing odds every year. Drought, floods, heat waves and late frosts, the wheat seemed to survive. The seeds were so densely packed with life, once they broke through the soil, not much could hinder them.

Chapter Four

The sound of a horn honking outside her old bedroom window the next morning pulled Chelsea from a deep sleep. There was something about being in her own bed, her face buried in sheets that smelled like fresh air and the breezy scent of the geraniums planted at the foot of the old fashioned clothes line.

Chelsea heard the screen door slam and rolled over to look out her window into the pre-dawn darkness. She saw her grandfather descend the stairs wearing his ancient blue jean jacket, carrying his thermos. She made out the form of an old blue pick-up in the drive, a man with a cowboy hat sat behind the wheel. She heard a couple of faint 'howdys' as Grandpa climbed into the truck, the door slammed, and it moved down the gravel drive and out onto the highway.

The clanking of pots and pans and smell of coffee told her that Gram was up. She imagined the older lady filling the red and green striped thermos and giving Grandpa a kiss as they said goodbye. She had seen the scene repeated so many times over the years that in her adolescent mind, she had lay in bed and planned to treat her husband the same way. Her grandparents never parted without a touch of some kind. Gram always said it was like setting an anchor before they set out into the sea of life. Smiling at the thought, Chelsea hunkered down under the thick quilt, and laid her head on her pillow. She had dreamed many dreams on that pillow. Dreams of being a fashion photographer in New York. Dreams of the man she would one day marry. She thought she had met that man the next year when she had met David Renault and fallen head over heels for the boy genius. What a mess that had turned out to be.

As she lay there quietly, still drowsy with sleep, what had happened in the last few months in the city faded away. Her heart was light and she savored the peace that had descended on her in the middle of the night. Everything was going to be alright. A sudden twinge, starting with a memory, causing her to involuntarily grimace, descended into her heart. She laid her hand on her heart and willed the pain away. No longer claiming it as her own, she locked it away like an old diary. She had survived. Now she planned to thrive. She was going to let her roots grow deep into this good Kansas soil for the next six weeks and soak up some of its goodness. Like a small child on Christmas morning, she threw off her covers, pulled on her robe and pink fuzzy slippers and went down to help Gram with breakfast.

"Good morning Gram," Chelsea said, pushing through the swinging door into the kitchen door, giving the older woman a kiss on the cheek and reaching for a box of cereal in the cabinet above the stove.

Chelsea settled herself in one of the old fashioned red vinyl kitchen chairs. She'd eaten a lot of pie while sitting at Gram's kitchen table discussing boyfriends, dances and college plans. The kitchen, decorated top to bottom in red and gold roosters had always been the center of her grandparents' home, a tribute to Gram's talents as a cook.

"What smells so good?" Chelsea asked, pouring the milk on her cereal and taking a bite of the crunchy wheat flakes. Wheat cereal was a staple at that table for all the years that Chelsea had lived here. Gramps said not to bite the hand that fed you, and the kitchen was full of wheat products of all kinds. Milk dribbled out of the corner of Chelsea's mouth, and she took a swipe at it with her napkin.

"Did you forget all your manners in the big city, missy?" Gram asked, her eyes sparkling with humor. She handed her granddaughter another napkin from the colorful rooster shaped napkin holder that was flanked by matching salt and pepper shakers.

Chelsea smiled and took the napkin. It was nice to be able to smile after the weeks of stress she had endured with the trial, marking each word she spoke, measuring each movement, so that the defense attorney couldn't take advantage of any misstep or misspoken word. She was free here. Free to be herself. No clients, no bosses, no newspaper reporters.

The newspaper reporters had been the worst. They followed her everywhere once her identity leaked out. If she never saw another reporter, it would be too soon for her. She took a few more bites of cereal and watched as Gram pulled a breakfast casserole out of the oven and stuck a knife in the center to test its doneness.

"How can I help?" Chelsea asked, pointing with her spoon at the home-made cinnamon rolls, biscuits, jam and butter on the table in front of her.

"This was the last thing that needed to be baked, and it looks done," Gram said, laying aside the knife and using two red rooster shaped pot holders to set it on the top of the stove. She paused, laid down the pot holders and turned to her granddaughter. "It's so good to have you home, Chelsea," she said, reaching out one more time with another welcome home hug. Chelsea gladly folded herself into her Grandmother's arms and held on tight. "Besides," she said, wiping a tear from the corner of her eye with a dish towel, "Grandpa was just getting set to come get you and drag you back."

Chelsea laughed, but could actually imagine the old red pickup pull up to the glass and chrome Gleason Pharmaceuticals high-rise to drag Chelsea out by her elbow. There had been many times in the past few weeks that she had wished that might happen. Her cereal finished, she rinsed her bowl and loaded it in the dishwasher. She wrapped a jar of strawberry freezer jam in a cotton dishcloth and laid it in the picnic basket Gram had ready and grabbing Gram's quilted rooster-shaped pot holders, Chelsea carefully slid the casserole off the top of the stove and into the two-handled casserole carrier. Adding serving spoons and butter knives, the ladies closed the basket, and Chelsea reached for the keys to the SUV.

"Are you sure you're ready to go?" Gram asked a twinkle in her eye. "I know people are going to be really glad to see you, but in that outfit, you may just be the talk of the town."

Chelsea looked down at her robe and pink fuzzy slippers. Laughter began to bubble up from her belly. Once it started, neither one could stop. They laughed until they were weak, Chelsea

Free to Fly

doubled over, tears streaming down her face. "Oh, I must have needed a good laugh," she said, wiping her eyes and tucking the strands of hair that had come loose back into the knot on the top of her head. Inside, she felt like a trickle of warm water had begun to flow over the dry rocks in the streambed of her soul. All at once she knew that this is what she'd been missing. She was home. It was as if a well had opened up in her heart.

Sobriety hit for a moment. The pain, never far from the surface, threated to escape the carefully crafted confines Chelsea had made for it. She had the sudden urge to tell Gram everything. The walking away from God, the rape and the aftermath. The wall of protection Chelsea had built slammed down on the idea. Not today. Today she was going to settle into the peace and love that was surrounding her. Today, she celebrated. She was back in Purchase. She knew God had something in mind for her here, but something inside her was afraid to hope. She felt as if her future was about to begin. What that would be, God only knew.

Taking the stairs two at a time, Chelsea felt lighter as she went to her room and changed her clothes. She pulled her light blue college sweatshirt over her head and slipped on her down vest to ward off the morning chill. Pulling on her jeans and old boots, she started to put the pink slippers under the bed. The slippers had been a gift from her best friend. The daughter of one of her grandmother's friends from church and older by four years, Chelsea remembered Maggie from church plays and youth group trips. She had known that Maggie had gotten a good job and moved away, but never dreamed they'd be roommates one day. It was Maggie who had helped her settle in and find a church when she first moved to St. Louis. Springy auburn hair and square freckled nose, Maggie had proved to be a great friend. She had introduced Chelsea to her own friends, and they had adopted her as one of their own. She'd discovered new restaurants and baseball under the lights. They'd attended church functions together and played board games that went well into the night. At least in the beginning. The church in St. Louis was quite large, and although the people were very nice, she missed the intimacy in the smaller Purchase Christian Church. She loved her friends, but her roots had always been in the country.

Maggie was a communicator and had taught Chelsea how to use the office messaging system and had her joining all of the social media sites. It was a level of connectedness that Chelsea wasn't used to. With all the new experiences of life in the big city and the level of commitment that her new job required, Chelsea had wandered away from her dependence on God.

Actually, when she looked back at it now, she knew that her wandering had begun in high school. She had given in to the pressure to go to parties with her friends where there was drinking and worse, and that had led to other things. She had begun a slow slide into her own will instead of God's perfect plan for her life. She had done things and met people that had brought destruction into her life, and that sin, like the Bible says, had eventually led to death. The death of the visions and dreams she believed her Heavenly Father had planned for her, and ultimately her decision to end the life of her child. If she had chosen to remain hooked to the vine, her life might not have turned out this way.

"A man's heart plans his way, but the Lord directs his steps."

Chelsea remembered that verse from her Sunday school class. If she had just let God plan her way and direct her steps, none of this would have happened.

She had come back to Him in that emergency room the night of the attack. She had felt swathed in His comfort and in His love as she had cried out to him, sorry for ignoring the still small voice that had told her not to go to the park that night, sorry for ignoring the whispers she had heard so often, calling her to prayer and to Bible study. She was sorry, now for the years she had wasted planning her own way. She knew there was no condemnation. He had been waiting for her with arms wide open.

She didn't always feel His comforting presence now, but she had the words He had left behind to guide her. Her Bible was never far from her side, a measuring rod for all her experiences, a treasure of wisdom, the bedrock of her growing sense of security and faith.

Never in a million years had she thought going into this mess that any good could have come out of it. She gave God thanks for the miracles he had done since the attack. She pulled her thick blonde hair into a pony tail and threaded it through the hole in the back of an old seed corn hat. Chelsea remembered the words that Gram had whispered to her in the hospital, in the early morning hours after the attack. "...*all things work together for good.*"

Chelsea had held Gram's hand and wished it was true. So many things had changed that night. The largest of which had brought her home.

Chapter Five

Chelsea bounded down the stairs and found her grandmother. She grabbed the picnic basket followed Gram to the barn, loading the basket in the back seat of their SUV to make the short trip to the Ross's. Climbing in the front passenger seat, Chelsea ran her hand over the black silt that lay like a fine layer over the dashboard of the truck. Home, she thought, rubbing the fine silt of the Kansas soil that settled into every crack and crevice this time of year between her fingers. Home is where the heart is, she thought, unconsciously laying her hand on her heart, leaving an exact imprint of her hand on her blue sweatshirt. She looked at her sweatshirt and then at Gram and the laughter and tears began to flow again. Gram seemed to be laughing at the humor in the situation and Chelsea laughing in relief, because she was home, where a little dirt didn't matter. She wiped her tears, dusted off as much dirt as possible, and determined to enjoy her day.

She looked in the distance and could see the sky on the horizon was filled with ochre wheat chaff. She opened her window to enjoy the clean fresh smell of the country and felt rigidity melt from her muscles that she hadn't realized was there. The peace that had descended on her in the night had something to do with her decision to leave Gleason Pharmaceuticals, she was sure of it.

Sometime in the middle of the night, she had realized that she no longer wanted to do her job as a sales representative. She wasn't giving up, but understood now that her heart had never really been in it.

It had sounded so glamorous at first. She had been fascinated by the chemistry classes she had taken at college. A recruiter had come to campus and offered her an exorbitant amount of money, an amount over six figures, the excitement of travel and meeting new people, and the satisfaction of providing medicine to help people heal. All these things had appealed to her burgeoning sense of freedom from the restrictions of small town life. She was ready to see what the world had to offer. She had seen it alright. Against her Grandfather's gentle advice and the whispers of that still small voice, she had packed up and left for the city.

Not that Grandpa had ever forbid her. He had known she had to lead her own life and make her own choices. He had, however, asked questions in order to make her think through her decision.

Her time in the city hadn't all been bad, she thought as she looked back over the past five years. She had learned to love some parts of the city. She had often taken a picnic lunch to the park near her job, and spent many hours at the botanical gardens and world class zoo. She realized now that what had attracted her were the wide open spaces of the botanical gardens, and the rich greens and golds of the trees that bordered the walkways throughout the zoo. The same colors she was seeing now as they drove past miles of golden fields defined on three sides by green hedge rows, the road sides cut with deep ditches, marked off like a ruler by dark brown telephone poles. In her high school years, she had spent hours with her camera in the fields around Purchase. She had watched as pheasants made their way out of the hedgerows and marsh hawks circled the combined fields, looking for their next meal of field mice or voles. The memories were sweet, and they chased to the back of her mind the ones she had come to Purchase to forget.

The rest of the drive was filled with quiet talk about neighbors, the harvest, and the upcoming church bazaar. As they turned into the gravel lane that led to the Ross's place, Chelsea could see tables were being set up and covered with brightly colored tablecloths. She knew the men had been working for a solid two hours, and it was time to break for breakfast, one of the three meals that would be provided by family and friends as the twelve hundred acre tract was cleared, and the remaining straw was cut and baled. The wheat was the cash crop, but the straw was the icing on the cake. The light, rectangular bales of wheat straw not only provided bedding for the farmer's animals and mulch for their gardens, but were fast becoming a popular building material for environmentally friendly homes.

"We're lucky the fields were far enough from the house it doesn't look like the chaff is going to be a problem," Gram said. Chelsea knew that even when the bits of shell around the wheat blew from the combine, the nuisance of burning eyes or nose was considered a small inconvenience. To them, it was a sign that all was well as the crop came into the barn.

"That's Dane Ross right there," Gram said pointing through the windshield to a tall, dark haired man with a straw cowboy hat. She ran through her mind the rest of what she knew about Dane Ross. Gram had written her that the man had wanted to be a preacher but his parents' lack of finances had led him to take a full-ride scholarship in engineering instead. She thought she remembered that he was still active in campus ministries as well as the youth group and occasionally filled the pulpit at the Purchase Community Church. As a matter of fact, now that she thought about it, she seemed to know a lot about the man who was a perfect stranger. Had Gram had something in mind when she had filled her last few letters with information about the younger Ross? She knew Gram and Gramps would be going to the heavily attended special service that was always held on the Sunday morning after the Harvest of Talents. Many of the out-of-towners were invited to the service as they shopped at the sale and the church was usually packed to overflowing. Chelsea supposed she'd have to go, although her heart really wasn't in it. It wasn't that she didn't love the people; she just wanted her privacy for a little longer. Some wounds were still fresh, and she didn't need any probing, not even the gentle, loving, kind that she had come to know in Purchase. Some things were best left unsaid. Some things, she knew, she would never uncover. She slid out of the SUV and opened the back door, reaching for the loaded picnic basket.

"Here, let me take that for you."

She jumped and nearly dropped the picnic basket at the sound of a male voice so close. She froze for a second to let her mind gain control of her reaction to run. She took a deep, steadying breath as the tall dark man put a hand out to steady the basket. She managed, with shaking hands to look up at the man in the cowboy hat and give him a tentative smile.

Realizing from her reaction what his offer to help had done, he immediately took two steps back. "I'm sorry," he said, standing quietly as he watched her re-gather herself. He watched as the panic drained away and was replaced by a glint of good humor. He relaxed and tried again. "Hello Chelsea. I'm Dane Ross. Your grandmother's told me a lot about you. Can I help you with your basket?" He made no move toward her until she nodded and held the basket out to him.

She recovered enough to give him a genuine smile. "I am Chelsea, and Gram seems to have told me a lot about you, too," she said, glancing at her Grandmother and wondering if that was a coincidence. She followed the cowboy as he carried the basket to the already heavily laden tables. He looked in his element, his long legs clad in dark blue jeans, a light blue work shirt with sleeves rolled up and straw cowboy hat. This must have been who picked up Grandpa this morning too, Chelsea thought, looking around for another cowboy-type hat in the crowd. All she could see was a field of brightly colored seed corn hats, and a few with the name of her grandfather's favorite tractor.

Taking a deep breath, Chelsea followed him as he led them to where the tables were already full of colorful casserole dishes. Paper plates, cups and napkins were being weighed down with anything handy to keep them from blowing away in the breeze as it blew across the wide open spaces surrounding the farm. It was the same breeze that kept curtains dancing in windows and houses cool all summer long. With a tip of his straw hat, Dane Ross retreated and the women began to set their food out on heavily laden tables. Huge urns of coffee were perking, and pitchers of orange juice were placed on tables, just in time for hungry farmers and their helpers.

A few minutes later, Chelsea glanced up to see Dane Ross looking at her from across the yard. Was that pity she saw in his eyes? She was not going to be pitied. Her face flushed, and her heart sank. The past was over, and she was determined it wasn't going to affect her future. She got busy uncovering casseroles and listening as neighbors talked about crop yields, children, and the upcoming church bazaar. She was comforted by the sights and sounds of the small farming community. Something about it made her shoulders relax. She was safe here.

She felt a slim arm slip around her waist and smelled the familiar scent of lavender.

"Lisbeth Renault," Chelsea said, turning to return the embrace. Lisbeth had been her best friend all through high school, and Chelsea had worked on her parent's tree farm every summer since she was old enough to work. Lisbeth was tall like her father but thin and fine boned like her mother, her pale freckled skin showing her English heritage. Simon and Margaret Renault, Lisbeth's great, great grandparents had come from England and brought with them rootstock from some of Europe's oldest trees. They settled in Kansas and planted the trees in hopes of making them thrive. Some species took hold, and others didn't, but using what they learned, the Renaults had become nationally known for growing and raising heritage trees. They owned some of the oldest pure rootstock in the country, and their trees commanded high prices through their website and catalog.

"How is your family, Lisbeth?" Che[lsea asked, eager for] news of her friend's large family. The Re[nault children had all] grown and out of the house except Lisb[eth, who had taken] over the business when her parent's r[etired. David was] back home finishing her internship at a v[...]

"David is back," Lisbeth said simply. "He wa[s offered] another job, and says he's back for good. He's living on the fa[rm,] setting up a new fancy computer system and basically getting in my way," she said, shaking her head and rolling her eyes.

Lisbeth was laughing, but Chelsea knew her well enough to know there was a thread of truth to what she was saying. Chelsea had dated Elisabeth's brother David for several years in high school. While Chelsea and the rest of the Renault children had worked on the family's heritage tree farm, David had stayed indoors working on the computer in his room. In the summers, he had rarely seen the light of day, preferring to work at night and sleep during the day. As his awards and success had grown, so had his ego. At first, Chelsea found his genius and single-mindedness attractive, but by the time David had left her behind for college, his work on his computers had become an obsession. Chelsea sighed and slid her arm through the crook of Lisbeth's.

"What happened with David is water under the bridge now, Lisbeth, and I forgave him a long time ago," Chelsea said, meaning every word of it. She had found that life was too short to carry around a grudge over a prom date.

"Great," Lisbeth said, giving her friend another hug. "Let's go grab some of your Gram's cinnamon rolls before this hoard eats them all. Then we can catch up."

a was glad for the company as they made their way the quickly filling tables. They found an empty spot and themselves at home, picking up their friendship as if no time passed in the years they'd been apart. Lisbeth asked about the trial, and when Chelsea began to share some of the details, tears of compassion rolled down her friend's cheeks. Searching for a tissue, Lisbeth emptied her purse, spilling its contents on the table.

"I prayed every night for you," Lisbeth said, "but I wish I could have done more."

"You did plenty," Chelsea said, stopping her friend's protest with a smile and a reassuring hand on her arm. "You called and sent e-mails. I was so thankful for my family and friends."

Changing the subject, Chelsea noticed a flash of pink baby booties on a small note-sized card in the pile of belongings Lisbeth had pulled from her purse. "Someone having a baby?" she asked, pulling the card from between wadded up tissues and her friend's billfold.

"My sister Jeanine," Lisbeth said smiling. "She's pregnant, but didn't want to marry Dean, the father. "She's finishing her last year at medical school, and then she's coming home to have the baby. Mom has agreed to watch the baby while Jeanine completes her residency. You'd think someone training to be a doctor would know how to prevent a pregnancy," Lisbeth said, shaking her head. "I'm sorry for her that it turned out this way, it's going to make her life a lot more complicated, at least until she gets her residency over and can get a good job. I have to agree that marrying the wrong man wasn't the right solution either.

Chelsea knew that whatever happened, Jeanine would need a lot of support. She determined right then to help any way she could. Thank God she had chosen to keep the baby. Tears shimmered in Chelsea's eyes as the pain of decision shot through her heart once again.

"The family wanted to give her a shower, and I know they'd love you to come. It's next Saturday at 3:00 at the farm," Lisbeth said.

Chelsea sniffed and then blew her nose and thought about the upcoming shower. That was the thing that Chelsea loved about the people in Purchase. Love covered a multitude of sins. They felt plenty free to tell you when they thought you were headed the wrong direction. Even Chelsea had been called to the carpet at Purchase Community Church in her younger days.

Lisbeth's mind must have been running in the same direction. "Remember the time Pastor Ben caught us sneaking around after dark with boys, smoking cigarettes behind the church? He made us come inside and talked to us about our worth. About how much God loves us, and our potential, and how running around with boys prematurely could lead us away from God's destiny for us?"

Chelsea thought back and realized that even during those years, God had been trying to keep her on the right path.

"Do you remember the time we were counselors at church camp and snuck out and went to the boy's counselor's cabin? I think back now and realize that even then God was protecting us. Who knows what would have happened if that candle hadn't caught the cabin curtains on fire." Lisbeth said. "I was grounded for a month. Straightened me right up, though. Bored the orneriness right out of me. We both kind of cooled our jets for a while after that," Lisbeth said, stuffing the contents of her purse back in the bag. "Remember when David came home from college to take you to the Junior prom, not because he wanted to, but because he had promised me we'd double date? What a disaster that turned out to be. He ruined the whole thing. He thought he was such a college hot shot," Lisbeth said, shaking her head.

Chelsea could laugh now, but it wasn't funny then. David had paid no attention to her the entire night, focused only on himself and telling anyone who would listen that he was big man on campus. She wasn't looking forward to seeing him if he did show up today, but it would seem out of character for the old David to do something for someone else. Unless he'd changed.

"Let's talk about what we're going to do now that you're home for a few weeks. Do you have much planned?"

"I'm planning to help Gram with canning and Gramps and I are going to paint the porch while I'm here, and I'd love to come to Jeanine's shower if I'm really invited."

"Of course you are. You're part of the family. You've probably planted and pruned as many trees as the rest of us have," Lisbeth said, giving her friend's hand a squeeze and motioning for her to keep the invitation. "Mom and the girls will love seeing you. Jeanine, of course will be there, and Connie. Banner and her husband are home for a few weeks, but will be heading back to the city soon. They've all come back for the shower and to help at the Harvest of Talents. In fact, when Mom heard you were back, she wondered if you'd be willing to help this weekend. She still has booth space available at the Harvest festival. I'm sure she would totally understand if you don't want to, but she wanted you to know that you'd be a blessing if you were interested in helping. Maybe make a few batches of cookies or a cake or two?"

"Of course I'd be willing to help," Chelsea said without thinking. "Gram and I talked last night, and I had already been thinking of donating a few photographs. I've just spent several weeks matting and framing some pictures I've taken over the years. Do you think anyone would be interested in those?"

"You know the people of Purchase, Chelsea. They'd love to see what you've done. You were always such a good photographer."

Chelsea felt herself blush at Lisbeth's praise and decided to get to work tonight on matting and framing the rest of her photos.

They threw their paper plates away and walked arm and arm toward the table where Lisbeth's mom was pouring coffee. Gloria Renault was delighted when Chelsea offered to help. The matronly lady assigned her half of the table that would hold her grandmother's pies. Chelsea was now a vendor at the biggest event of the year, the Purchase Community Church Harvest of Talents. So much for privacy for a few days, she thought. Everyone in town and beyond would be there. What was done was done. Besides, it was really a good cause. Maybe having her photos framed and ready to sell was another small way of bringing good from the negative of the rape and trial. She would have never taken the time to mat and frame the photos if she hadn't been forced into seclusion during the trial.

Their conversation ended with hugs and promises to see each other tomorrow. Chelsea continued to help, moving around the tables, putting away leftovers, matching empty plastic containers to lids. Her eyes wandered over the crowd until she found the back of Dane Ross's head. He turned and looked toward her, as if he had felt her gaze. Humor crinkled the corners of his eyes as he laughed with a group of men over the last sips of coffee. The only thing better than the pies made by the Purchase women were the stories told by the men, her Grandpa always said. The oral history of Purchase had been handed down for years by men sipping coffee. The history of the town and its people evolved depending on who was doing the telling and how many tellings the story had gone through.

His laughter dissolved as their eyes met, and the look of compassion turned Dane's features serious. Maybe it wasn't pity she had seen. Maybe she had jumped to conclusions. She smiled and nodded as then side-stepped as two squealing toddlers and a dog chased each other around her legs, nearly knocking her over. Chelsea smiled at the children and thought of her of Gram's words, "As long as there are children on this earth, there will always be laughter." Chelsea believed that laughter would again become a natural part of her life. She had already laughed more in the two days she'd been home than she had for the last few years. She couldn't figure out what had kept her away so long. Pride she supposed. Not wanting to admit her mistakes. She vowed never to let that happen again. She couldn't see how it was going to all work out yet, but sometimes you had to believe in things you couldn't see.

She collected paper plates and napkins, and headed to the trash can and the group of ladies gathered there. She fell into the natural rhythms of conversation about who was bringing what to the Harvest of Talents. It felt right to be home.

"She's pretty," Pop Ross said, cocking his head first toward Chelsea and then toward his bachelor son.

"Which one?" Dane asked, pretending innocence.

"Which one?" his father asked, his eyebrow raised in skepticism.

Dane knew exactly which woman his father was talking about, but he refused to take the bait. He ignored his father's comment and searched the man's face for signs of fatigue. He stepped up on the porch and looked at the older man's eyes, hoping he wasn't overdoing it.

"Imagine all these people doing this just for me," Pops Ross said, taking off his cap and running his good hand through his thinning hair. Replacing his cap, he put his hand on his son's shoulder to steady himself as they walked carefully down the steps into the front yard that was teeming with neighbors and friends.

"You've done it for them, Pops," Dane said, his arm steadying the still recovering older man. "You should take it easy. You lost a lot of blood." A small shudder went through Dane's body at the thought of what might have been. The emergency room doctor had said that if the ambulance had arrived five minutes later, the older man might not have made it. As it was, the surgical team had fought for twelve hours in surgery to reattach the arm and two weeks in the hospital fighting infection. Dane wasn't about to let his dad's health backslide now.

He breathed a thanksgiving prayer, again thanking God for saving his Dad. He had no guilt over the accident or leaving Pops alone to run the farm. He knew God had called him to something besides farming. Twelve hundred acres wasn't enough to support two families, not that family was even on Dane's horizon. He did wonder sometimes if his father was lonely. Dane, himself, felt fulfilled at his job, and his volunteer work at the university and the Purchase Community Church. He particularly liked to fill the pulpit when the regular pastor was gone. He was already looking forward to preaching the extra service tomorrow for the Harvest of Talents. He had already begun seeking God for a word. He also enjoyed working with the youth, although at times he had to do what his dad called, "pulling a few tails." One of the tails he had pulled recently belonged to a young man named Josh Wagner. His mom, Lisa, had come to the church last month to ask for his advice. The petite, dark haired woman had come into the office and immediately burst into tears.

"I'm sorry to be like this, but I've heard rumors that Josh is smoking and drinking and running with the wrong crowd," she said through muffled her sobs. I've tried talking to him, but he won't listen to me. I know he still has some issues because his father left us, but I'm at a loss as to what to do." Her shoulders were shaking with the sobs, and Dane longed to comfort the woman. He hoped his gentle reassurance would be enough, because although he wanted to put his arm around the weeping woman, he couldn't. His training and good sense told him to lead her to the One who could do her the most good. And that's what he did. He told her about her Father's love for her, and that he sent His Son as a sacrifice, a bridge, from people who weren't holy to the One who is. He also gave her pamphlets on how to talk to Josh about the dangers of smoking and drinking, and vowed to talk to the boy himself. She had listened carefully to the seeds he had planted, and

Free to Fly

although she had said she wanted to think about all he had said, he believed it wouldn't be long before she had a personal Savior too.

A week after their talk, he had invited Josh along on a youth group camping trip. One night over the campfire he used the same pamphlets he had given Josh's mom as he explained the dangers of gateway drugs. He hadn't been harsh, but he had been firm. He had also mentioned that the youth group crowd was probably a better bunch to hang out with than the one's Josh was running with now. Dane hoped the straight talk and compassion may have turned the trick, but it was too early to tell. Josh had come with his mom this morning to help move grain, and Dane thought that was a good sign. He'd make it a point to thank him for coming.

As the day wore on, the fields were cleared and straw bales bucked from hay racks to the hayloft by strong, sunburned teenagers. Dane moved through the farmers, shaking hands and thanking them for being there for Pops. It wouldn't be hard to come up with a message for Sunday's Harvest of Talent service. He had witnessed a living sermon today. The farmers left one by one until finally he and Pop waved goodbye to the last pickup truck loaded with the tables and chairs that went back to the Purchase Church basement. The two men sat rocking on the front porch, drinking a final glass of tea for the evening. They talked about the goodness of God, and the spirit of care and concern of their neighbors that had enveloped them all that day. As the sun set, Dane said his good night and went to his room to work on his message, putting his thoughts of thanks to the community down on paper.

Chapter Six

The next day dawned clear and bright, the sunshine a perfect backdrop for the Harvest of Talents.

"Let me help you with that, Gram," Chelsea said, unloading more pies from their carriers and placing them on the eight foot table next to her own display of carefully arranged framed photos. Each pie was marked with its price and flavor, and Chelsea had typed out stories for each of her photos on three by five cards and placed them on the table.

Gram reached over to take a donation as a gooseberry pie changed hands and Chelsea reached for her camera.

"Thank you for coming," Gram said with a smile as she put the money in the cash box. "Your ten dollars will help feed a family this winter."

Chelsea snapped a photo of the exchange. She could almost feel the pleasure of God in what was taking place today. She took a deep breath and looked around at the people who were using their gifts and talents to help take care of those less fortunate.

She knew that the picture she had just taken was a good one. She only hoped others would appreciate her work enough to help support the food bank. At first, a thought, like a dark cloud that shrouded her mind, that maybe shoppers were buying her photos out of pity. She shook off that thought as people seemed to truly enjoy her reminders of life in Purchase and the beauty of nature. Sales that morning had been brisk. Chelsea had seriously considered going into photography as a career after high school, and by the way things were selling today, she probably could have been successful.

Chelsea's stomach rumbled and she realized it was time for a break. It had been a busy morning, and she unconsciously looked to see how high the sun was in the sky. It was funny that never once had she tipped her head back to find out what time it was in the city, but here she knew her neighbors would all do the same thing.

She was looking forward to getting off her feet and taking a break for lunch. She could see the lunchtime replacements making their way toward her table. She gave Lisbeth's sister Banner a big hug as she walked up to the table to relieve them. She walked with Gram to the tent where the women of the church were serving lunch. They sat at the table, enjoying the ham and beans and cornbread and the warm sunshine that had settled around them. By the size of the crowd, it looked like the day was going to be a success.

Chelsea felt a cool breeze on her legs and heard the wind stir in the trees. It reminded her of the cold air that rolled in before a thunderstorm. She looked at the horizon to check for dark clouds, but saw none. The nice thing about living in the middle of tornado alley was that Kansas was flat enough that you could usually see a storm coming for miles. She had just sat back on her bench and relaxed when she saw jeans clad legs appear next to her out of the corner of her eye. A slight rise in her blood pressure, but nothing she couldn't handle. She looked up to see the smiling face of Dane Ross. Her pulse began to slow.

"Would you ladies mind some company?" Dane asked, waiting for an invitation before making himself comfortable.

Chelsea let out the breath she had been holding and scooted over to offer a place at their table. "Preacher Dane Ross tomorrow, I hear," she said, taking another bite of the warm cherry cobbler that been delivered to their table.

"I am," he said, settling his long legs under the paper covered table.

Something about Dane Ross caused her to relax. Being around him was comfortable. Gentle was the word that had come to mind, but strong. As she looked at him, she imagined he could be fiercely protective of anyone he loved. Suddenly, she realized where her thoughts had gone, and that Dane had been talking to her. It had something to do with her photos. She could feel her face flush as she realized she had no idea what he had said.

Gram looked at her, a protective glance, and then back at Dane. "I think it might be a little early yet for something like that," she said, eyes imploring Chelsea to "just say no."

Chelsea looked at her Grandma and then back at Dane. "What did you just say?" she asked, more confused by Gram's strong reaction than anything.

"I said, I was wondering if you would allow me to use your photo, and your story of the butterfly as an example at tomorrow morning's service."

Chelsea remembered the photo. It was one of her favorites, one that held special meaning for her. A beautiful golden butterfly perched delicately on the tip of a golden flower. When she had seen the developed picture, Chelsea had thought about how the petals of the flower had seemed to reach up to surround the delicately balanced butterfly, to keep it from falling too far. She had seen it as a picture of her Father's love. How He was always there to catch us if we fall. Her heart ached at the knowledge that she had fallen. Hard...

Chelsea digested Dane's words about using the photo in the service and leaped up from the table. "I'm nobody's example," she said, turning on her heel and hurrying toward the SUV.

Gram got up to follow Chelsea, gave Dane an apologetic look, and left him standing, wondering what he had done to cause such a reaction. Dragging up her past was probably the last thing she wanted to do. His insensitivity seemed to know no bounds. Hat in hand, he walked over to Chelsea's table, hoping to get a clue as to how to undo the damage he had just done.

He took out a twenty dollar bill and picked up the picture of the delicate, golden butterfly. He had meant to help but he had obviously caused harm. The best thing to do might just be to stay away from her. Somehow, though, he felt drawn. Her delicate features came back to mind as he walked to his truck. He had seen pain in her eyes, but for a moment he had also seen shame. He walked to his truck, opened the door and rested his booted foot on the running board as he ran the conversation back in his mind, trying to figure out what he had said to upset her.

He had read that sometimes rape victims thought that somehow it was their fault. If that's what Chelsea was dealing with, he hoped he might be able to find a way to dispel the notion. Why he thought he needed to help her, he didn't know. He knew he felt some kind of connection. Certainly empathy. He also knew her heart was badly bruised. He had watched, off and on, during the day as she gently laid her hand over her heart. He had seen that before, in women who had lost their husbands after fifty years of marriage, and wives of men who were lost at war. It was the universal sign of heartbreak and he knew it well. He started the truck and headed toward the church to finish his message for tonight. All the while, the face of the sweet Kansas farm girl was never far from his mind.

Chelsea pulled herself together and recovered enough that by the time Gram found her, she was ready to go back to her table. But only after she was sure Dane had gone. She wasn't sure why she had over-reacted so badly. Her emotions seemed to have a life of their own lately. And she didn't know how much she had given away about her secret. For the first time, Chelsea wondered what the good people of Purchase Community Church would think if they knew she had taken the life of her own baby. She reached again to cover her heart. This time, her hand dropped a little lower, as if the emptiness of her womb was apparent to those around her.

Telling Gram she didn't feel well, she took the keys to the SUV and drove back to her grandparent's farm. She never should have come back to Purchase. They knew her too well. Something would slip out. Something she was determined to hide. She was tempted to pack her things and leave. Instead, she went up to her room, rolled up in the comforter on her bed and, got out her Bible and opened to her favorite scripture.

"Many waters cannot quench love, Nor can the floods down it..."

Chelsea's heart began to quiet as the song about God's love calmed the storm in her heart. "Will I ever be free of this pain, God?" Chelsea asked, knowing her heavenly Father cared for her.

"Come to me, all you who labor and are heavy laden, and I will give you rest..."

Chelsea did just that. She lifted the burden off her soul and gave it to God. Even as God's comfort settled, she knew it was a temporary fix. She knew she needed help, but could think of no one she could ask. She loved her Gram, but how could she tell her Grandmother she had lost a great grandchild she would never know? Just the thought weighed on Chelsea's heart. She couldn't ask the people at church. They had a grief counseling group, but how could Chelsea explain her grief? The word exploded in her heart and a river of pure revelation flooded her mind. Thank you, God. This struggle to control her emotions and to look forward to tomorrow had a name. Why didn't someone tell her about the after-effects of losing a child? It was supposed to be a simple procedure, painless. No consequences. The more Chelsea thought about it, the more far-reaching the consequences were. She wept at her own failure, and for her baby, and for the injustice of it all.

Emotions spent, she laid her head down on her pillow and slept. The one-word gift from God helped her understand her emotional turmoil. She was going to have to trust Him to send help. There was something so basic and primal about having no one else to go to. It assured her she could fall on the Rock.

She dozed lightly and awakened when she heard her bedroom door open. The hallway light filled the crack. She didn't feel like talking, so she lay quietly, giving no indication she was awake. The door closed softly and she heard sock-covered feet pad away, leaving the lingering scent of sunshine and hard work. Grandpa Pete. Her heart warmed as she felt his love and care. She pulled her covers closer and relaxed into a dreamless sleep. Tomorrow was going to be a new day, and the warmth in her heart and the song in her spirit assured her everything was going to be alright.

Chapter Seven

Dane shuffled through the newspapers in the back room of the library. The library kept the back issues until they had time to scan the information into the computers. He was re-reading the newspaper accounts of Chelsea's attack and trial. No one should have to go through this kind of treatment, Dane thought. The newspapers had made the trial into a sideshow. The muscle in his jaw twitched as he tried to contain his anger. Still, something about the timing of Chelsea's return to Purchase was bothering him. The trial had been over for a few weeks before she had left the city. What was it that had finally driven her home? He straightened and refolded the papers under the watchful eye of the librarian who was not at all happy with his choice of reading material. He had to hand it to the community of Purchase, if the look the librarian was giving him was any indication, the town certainly protected their own. Now, he supposed, word of his interest in Chelsea's case would probably travel down the aisles of the library, into the neighboring beauty shop and on to the café. So be it. If people wanted to know what his interest was in Chelsea James, he could honestly say he was concerned about her. As a matter of fact, he could hardly stop thinking about her. He restacked the newspaper gave the librarian a friendly smile as he walked out into the bright morning sunshine.

Chelsea slept late after the emotional turmoil at the Harvest of Talents. What must people think of her? Probably only concerned and praying for her, she thought. She pulled her hair to the top of her head, and put on her robe and ever-present slippers. Brushing her teeth, she looked at the sad girl in the mirror, and wondered how she got that way.

"There is no shadow of turning in me . . ."

The words blew though Chelsea like a breath of wind. Of course, none of this was God's doing. She had never really blamed him, even about the rape. Bad things happen. They had just never happened to her. She looked out through the gauze curtains to see bright sunshine and a blue sky with puffy clouds promising another beautiful day in the heartland.

Enough soul-searching for the day. She could smell coffee brewing. It reminded her of all the times the family had spent the night Kansas City to be awakened by the smell of freshly roasted coffee in their room. That same rich aroma of roasted coffee still came to mind when she saw the ground and bagged coffee on the grocery store shelves. Chelsea chose to dwell on those good memories for a moment. She tightened her robe and padded down the stairs and through the swinging door to the kitchen. There, to her surprise, sat Gram, Grandpa and a very sheepish looking Dane Ross. No doubt he was surprised by her sleepy-eyed ragamuffin look. Chelsea felt her face flush. Grandpa Pete straightened up from leaning on the counter, coffee cup in hand and cleared his throat. By the look in his eyes, Chelsea was almost sure they had been talking about her.

Gram looked somewhat apologetically at her granddaughter, then brightened and offered her a cup of coffee. "Dane came to bring back our things from the sale," she said, explaining Dane's presence in the kitchen.

Dane pointed to the stack of pie pans and dishes left from the ham and bean supper. "I just thought I'd drop those by before I headed to the church."

He looked good in a navy blue polo and tan khakis, his dark curls still damp from the shower. Services at Purchase Community Church were casual, and other than the choir robes, no one really tried to look official. Pastor Green's theory was that we were all kings and priests and we didn't need a go-between in a robe to get to heaven.

Her hand reached involuntarily to the mess of hair on top of her head. She telegraphed Grandpa a look that asked why didn't someone warn her? He shrugged his shoulders as if to say 'don't blame me'. He was no help. She gave Dane what she hoped was a dazzling smile and retreated up the stairs without her cup of coffee. She rolled her eyes and grabbed her things and headed to take a shower. She wasn't going to be grouchy. It was a beautiful day, and she was going to enjoy it. Coffee or not. After a hasty shower, she pulled on a pair of off white jeans and a bright yellow sweater set. She wasn't ready to give up on summer yet. She slid her feet into a pair of brown flats and checked her hair once more in the mirror. She had decided to leave her hair down, a shield in case her emotions, any one of many, over ruled her again. By the time she went back downstairs, Dane was gone, and Grandpa was pulling the car out of the barn.

"Would you like to wait a few minutes before we go, so we can slip in after the service starts?" Gram asked.

Chelsea looked the clock in the kitchen and realized they weren't going to get there any too early anyway. "We should be fine. I do have a lot of things to do this afternoon though and I wouldn't mind leaving right after service is over," she said, pouring a cup of coffee in a travel mug, and then walking arm in arm with her Grandmother to the waiting SUV.

As they approached the church, they could hear guitar music. They found seats near the back, and sang along with the words of the song on the screen above the platform. Chelsea's comfort level grew, and she relaxed as Dane walked onto the platform, with a confident smile, his Bible open in his hands.

"Blessed are the merciful, For they shall obtain mercy," Dane quoted. "I think a lot of you sitting out there today can expect a lot of mercy in the next few weeks. You were merciful to my father, who many of you know was injured in a farming accident. Most of you came and spent the day harvesting his fields for the price of a few delicious meals. Those of you who cooked and served those meals have been merciful to my family this weekend, and I thank God for you." Dane paused and looked one by one at the faces he had seen at the farm on Friday. Faces that had been extensions of God's loving hands toward his father.

"Blessed are the poor in spirit, For theirs is the kingdom of heaven," Dane read from the Bible laying open in his hand. Thank you to those who ministered the Kingdom of Heaven to my father yesterday. I have to tell you that it wasn't easy for him to accept that gift. We men are notorious for wanting to do everything ourselves. We're a proud bunch, generally. Our pastor once said that the poor in spirit are the ones that are humble. They're humble enough to accept the gift of God's Kingdom when it's offered to them in the hands of neighbors and friends like you. I know my father couldn't have done what was done yesterday all by himself. It took him realizing that you all were God's gift to him to receive the help, and for that, I'm also grateful. Sometimes, we can have a problem and struggle for years and never tell a soul. When we do that, we're hiding from whatever help God may want to bring us." Dane paused to let that message sink in. "If there's anyone here that feels burdened by something, and can't find a way to share it with someone, I'd like you to know that you don't have to feel alone. Look around you. There are people, including myself that are waiting to help bring the Kingdom of Heaven into your situation."

Chelsea looked around the small white sanctuary and knew that Dane was right. As she looked from face to face, she realized that these people would all be there for her, in any situation. They had proved it with their calls and letters and cards during the trial.

"*Blessed are those who mourn, For they shall be comforted. . .*"

Chelsea felt more than heard the words as they applied themselves to her heart like a balm. She felt His comfort wash over her again and sat quietly soaking up the love that had filled the small church. She was just bringing her attention back to Dane's sermon when he closed his Bible and began to pray a blessing over the people and a popular praise song began to play, and she had no trouble adding her voice in thanks. They would get through this, she and God.

Dane then announced the final total for the Harvest of Talents to a rousing round of applause. They had raised over $23,000 in one day. It would be enough finances to fund the food bank through the winter and well into the spring. Chelsea had been glad to learn that all of her photos had sold and had added a sizeable amount to the total. The service ended with another song, and Gran, Gram and Chelsea slipped out of their pew and out the doors, making their way to the SUV.

"Chelsea. Chelsea Livingston," a voice called from the front steps of the church.

Not wanting to delay their departure, Chelsea turned around, ready to be polite but firm. She was delighted when she saw the normally disheveled Mr. Frank, her high school photography teacher in hot pursuit, his brown suit coat flapping open, his tie slightly askew as he jogged down the sidewalk towards Chelsea.

"My gosh girl, it's good to see you," the editor said as he put an arm around Chelsea's shoulder, giving her a hug like the friend and mentor he had been during her high school years. Mr. Frank had been the one to show her how to frame photos, using the right speeds and exposures. She had won several prizes for her pictures during high school.

Tears formed in Chelsea's eyes as she stepped back and looked at his beaming face. "Mr. Frank, it's wonderful to see you."

He looked at her face a beat too long, and Chelsea thought she saw the familiar sympathy flash in his eyes. "It's good to have you

Free to Fly

back, Chels," he said, putting on a smile and nodding a friendly hello to her grandparents. "I saw your photos in the sale yesterday, and I was wondering if I could hire the local talent while she's home visiting."

Chelsea felt her heart leap in her body, instantly excited about the opportunity. She stopped herself long enough to wonder if this was something the Lord wanted her to do. No more running off on her own. "Thank you so much for the offer, Mr. Frank. What would you need me to do?" Chelsea asked.

"We need someone to take pictures for human interest pieces. We also need someone to take pictures of local color, and of some social events. It would only be the jobs you're interested in. We have a regular photographer for the rest."

Frank looked expectantly at Chelsea. She could feel herself being tempted. A chance to take pictures for a living. Chelsea almost jumped in with both feet.

Gram put a hand on Chelsea's arm as if to tell her to slow down. She didn't have to worry. Chelsea would only be here for a three or four more weeks, hardly long enough to start a new career.

"I'm sorry Mr. Frank," Chelsea said, "I'll only be here for a few more weeks."

The older man smiled and patted her arm. "We'll take as many pictures as you want to give us as long as you're here. I've seen your work Chelsea, and it's good. Fifty dollars every time one's printed."

Chelsea could hardly believe it. Getting paid to do the thing she loved the most, even if it was for only three weeks. She felt a release in her heart that this was an opening that God would have her walk through. She agreed to meet Frank at the newspaper office the next day to fill out the paperwork. Their drive back to the farm was pleasant as Grandpa drove, Gram's lips moved in silent prayer and Chelsea dreamed.

Chapter Eight

A week later, Chelsea walked to the Renault's farm next door and sat on the bench by the pond that was full of cattails, bullfrogs and pan fish. St. Louis seemed farther and farther away with each passing day. Her contentment grew and she felt a deep sense of peace begin to settle over her heart. It was as if bands that had constricted her in her old job popped, and she was released into a creative frenzy. She had felt her soul expand with each picture. She had sat on the hard wooden fences that surrounded her grandparents' acres and watched as Marsh hawks took to the air, skimming lightly over the fields, tilting from side to side in an airborne ballet. She saw pheasants run, and envisioned the annual migration of water fowl that would bring thousands of geese, ducks, and even an occasional crane to forage the small ponds and fields of the Kansas plains. She let her mind slip, as she sat on a tree stump, watching as the doves came in to settle for the night. The high Kansas sky had changed from pale blue to gold to velvety red as the stars began to appear on the opposite horizon. She pulled her light sweater closer to her body, and wished she could just fade into the Kansas sky. If only she could do that. Just fade away and pretend this all didn't happen. She rested her head on her knees, and let the sorrow trickle out in the form of tears.

"Weeping may endure for a night, But joy comes in the morning..."

Chelsea drew comfort from the words, and wondered what people did who didn't have a Heavenly Father they could rely on.

A covey of doves flushed from a nearby tree, causing her pulse to rise. Some small predator, she told herself. Fox or possibly coyote, moving in the semi-darkness, ready to start their evening rounds, re-marking their boundaries and searching for something to eat. Branches crackled in the hedge row behind her, and Chelsea tensed involuntarily. Fighting the urge to turn and look, she concentrated on keeping her breathing even. "Hello," a male voice said from several yards behind her.

Willing her body to stay calm as thoughts rifled through her mind, sorting them as they went, picking out what was true from the flight instinct that wanted her to bolt from her seat. Her shoulders relaxed significantly as her mind came up with the owner of the voice. It was a friend.

"Hello back," she said in a voice she hoped was close to normal. She heard the footsteps come closer, but still didn't turn around to look. She had to begin to trust. Besides, she didn't want him to see the tear marks on her face. She wiped her face with her sleeve, and hoped the near darkness would conceal the rest. "What brings you out in the woods this time of night?" she asked, wiping her hands on her jeans. Turning to face him, she saw a look in his eyes that she couldn't quite place. Was he be worried about her?

"Your grandfather said you had walked out this way a couple of hours ago. He seemed relieved when I offered to come find you," he said, motioning to the bench beside her. She nodded, and he sat down, tossing a piece of wheat stalk into the still waters of the pond.

Gramps was worried, that explained it. He had sent Dane to find her. "I lost track of time," she said, turning back to her seat, "and then stayed to watch an amazing sunset. I took lots of pictures. I'm hoping one of them might be good enough for the front page. Mr. Frank likes to put some good news on the front page occasionally, to balance out the car accidents, and arguments of the town board."

Dane laughed at the thought of the continual friendly antagonism between the members of the Purchase town council. A report of their good natured bickering often made its way to the editorial page in the *Purchase Daily News*. He supposed most small towns were like that, and had even considered running for the board himself at one time. Though he would have loved to serve in that capacity, he would have to move from his place in Salina, and he hadn't seen any real need. Yet. With his father getting older, the thought of moving had occurred to him. Most of his design work was computerized and could be done from anywhere there was internet service and cell phone reception.

He looked at the beautiful woman sitting beside him and lifted a hand to wipe away the remnants of her tears, but stopped himself. After his previous mistakes, he was determined to take it slow. "You almost ready to head back in?" he asked, burying his hands in his pockets, pretending to look at the remnant of light on the horizon. He wasn't looking anywhere, only away from her tear-stained cheeks. His fists clenched, still safely in his pockets. He would like to get his hands on that guy. As quickly as the thought came, it left. If Chelsea could forgive her attacker, as Sharon Livingston had told him she had, surely he could do the same.

They turned and walked through the tall prairie grass back to toward the back porch light and the light in the kitchen windows each one savoring the end of a perfect Kansas day, and quietly enjoying each other's company. Sometimes words weren't necessary. Sometimes, they weren't needed at all. Though several feet apart, he wanted to take her hand and offer whatever comfort he could. He didn't. He'd have to wait for the right time, if it ever came. He reminded himself that she had only promised to stay a few more weeks.

She thanked Dane for walking her home and searching for her grandparents, found them on the front porch watching the dust settle behind Dane's truck from the light of the vapor light on a tall pole along the drive.

"Sure could use a good rain," Gramps said, ever-present wheat straw between his teeth, watching as Dane drove away. "Settle the dust," he added. "A couple of fall storms and a good snow cover and the fields'll be perfect for the seed to winter over into spring. We'll be planting in a couple of months," he said, his musings spoken to no one in particular.

Planting time was fun on the farm, the promise of new seeds in the ground, but as a child, Chelsea had always looked forward to the burning of the wheat stubble on the farm. Every fire department in a three state radius was on alert once the burning started. Winds had been known to carry the fires across interstates, closing down traffic for hours. Chelsea recalled the thrill of miles of controlled burns that killed lingering pests and prepared the soil for planting. She knew that home was close when the signs on I-70 began to warn drivers to watch for smoke on the highway.

"We need to burn the fields here 'purty quick, before the weed seeds take hold," he added.

Chelsea had the feeling that Grandpa was delivering a message. She felt as if her stubble and chaff had been burned to the ground. She only hoped the crop that came up was new and green. She was ready to grow again.

After giving each of them a quick kiss, they said their goodnights and she retreated upstairs. The exercise had done her good. She was pleasantly relaxed as she took a bath in the old claw foot tub, and after drying her hair, rolled into bed.

She took out her Bible and considered just how the last few months had affected her life. The rape had been like a pebble dropped into the still, clear water of her life, and before it was all said and done, its ripples would wash over into many more lives. Her baby's for one. She knew the baby was with God, and she knew that heaven must be a really good place to be, but she grieved for what she'd never know. Was it a boy or girl? She sensed that it had been a boy, but could never really prove it. Call it mother's intuition. That thought sent an arrow piercing deep into her heart. She had been a mother. Fresh tears came, some of sorrow, some of joy. For a brief moment, she felt what millions of women felt. Whether hormonal flush, or spiritual attachment, she didn't know, but her breath was taken away by the wonder of conception. Although hers was by all accounts the very worst way to conceive, there had been a baby, a very little, tiny bit of a baby, but fruit of her body, none the less. She held her hand over the place where she had conceived, and felt a sense of wonder. A life. She let her mind linger on what the child would have looked like, letting the rippling in the water of her soul bring up the ache, and let her look at it. She allowed herself to look at it from several angles. She knew she was forgiven. She knew her baby was safe. The ripples of her choice expanded, as she wondered again, what Gram and Grandpa would think if they found out.

When my father and mother forsake me, Then the Lord will take care me . . .

Chelsea read the scripture again, this time through blurred eyes. She couldn't believe that her grandparents would act that way, but she had heard of other women who had lost everything when an abortion was uncovered. The thought of revealing her secret to anyone sent a shudder down her spine. One face floated up in her mind. Dane Ross. She had sensed his compassion several times, like tonight, but he was a complete stranger. No way was she going to unload this emotional bombshell on a stranger. She read for a few more minutes about God's amazing love for her, and comfort poured like honey over her heart as she turned out the light and rested her head on her pillow. Tomorrow will be a new day . . .

Chapter Nine

Dane found himself at the local library again, looking up the local media reports of the capture of Chelsea's attacker. He noticed that the trial had ended several weeks before Chelsea came home. What made her wait so long, he wondered? Surely she would have wanted to escape the spot light as soon as possible. Maybe she had things she needed to wrap up at work. Whatever it was, Pops had said that the whole town had let out a collective sigh of relief when she came home. One of theirs had been hurt. It was up to them to make sure it didn't happen again.

Dane checked out two books on rape counseling, and was given a curious look by the octogenarian librarian. It looked like a mild warning, mixed with curiosity, but he wasn't sure. Yes, the people of Purchase certainly seemed to look out for each other. He intended to carry on the tradition. The look of shame in Chelsea's eyes haunted him. He would pray and wait, and see what God would have him to do.

"I was saying," said a loud voice, "why don't you mind your own business? The lady was talking to me!"

Chelsea overheard the conversation as she stood in line at the post office mailing a package for her grandmother.

She was almost sure the two men arguing in the Purchase post office were members of the city council. A good-natured constituent standing behind Chelsea in the same line had raised a question about garbage disposal in town, and an argument had ensued. It never descended to real name calling, but often times the relative number of years each family had been in Pine County was mentioned, as if longevity itself had something to do with one's ability to make good decisions.

Chelsea smiled and paid for her package. She could envision the front page of the newspaper tomorrow. Something about garbage disposal, the pros and cons. Ten years ago, everyone just burned their garbage in burn barrels, but government regulations had put a stop to that. The discussion had been going on since then, whether the city should provide trash pickup, or residents should hire it done themselves. Chelsea smiled at the familiarity of the scene as she bought some stamps for Gram and collected her change.

She and Gramps spent that night watching one of his favorite movies on DVD. Chelsea popped some popcorn, curled up on the floral print couch pulling a quilt over her legs. Gramps chose his worn, leather recliner and within fifteen minutes appeared to be sound asleep. Chelsea watched the movie until the DVD began to act up. The picture broke up into small square pieces, and then broke down altogether. Pixelated was what she called it when it had happened at home. The same thing had happened to some of her photos. They were broken down in small pieces, and when they were put back together again in the photo lab, they were never quite the same.

She pulled the quilt under her chin, and wondered if that's what had happened to her. She had been broken down to small pieces by the rape and resulting loss of her child. She wondered if she'd ever really come back together again the way she was before it all happened. Maybe, like Gram said, it's the trials that make us strong. She hoped so. She had a new future to build. Chelsea left the popcorn in the bowl, and turned off the DVD player. She covered her grandfather's stocking feet with the quilt and kissed him lightly on the forehead. She thought she saw his eyes flutter open for a second, but maybe she just imagined it. As she turned to leave, he reached out his hand, and captured one of hers.

"You know we're here if you want to talk about anything, Sweet Pea," he said, holding her hand gently, reassuring her that she wasn't alone.

Chelsea's heart melted and she bent down to place another kiss on the top of his head. "I know, Grandpa. I know." She returned his squeeze and turned away, willing the tears to hold off until she got up the stairs and into her room. Chelsea held her hand over her chest and struggled to hold back the tears. It was becoming almost as painful to hold the secret in as she imagined it would be to share it. She knew that she had done the right thing in coming home. What the next step in the plan would be, she wasn't sure.

Chapter Ten

"Pickles," Chelsea said, identifying the sweet, spicy scent before she even entered the old fashioned kitchen, its wallpaper covered with roosters, mirroring the rooster salt and pepper shakers and kitchen towels. Rooster plates of various sizes and colors lined the rack that bordered one of the kitchen's walls. Grandpa had made the rack one Christmas, and it had been gathering plates ever since.

A pot of the last of the season's cucumbers boiled on the stove in pickling spices and brine, waiting to be poured into the hot jars and seals that were waiting in a shallow pan on top of the stove.

Memories of her mother, standing at this same stove, blending spices and jarring pickles filled Chelsea's mind. At seven, she had been too young to help, but she had sat at the enameled white table on one of the red vinyl covered chairs and listened to the adults talk about babies, and green beans and her father's new promotion. Her parents had been traveling back from house hunting in Tulsa when the accident happened. Chelsea had lost the little sister she had never known in that accident also. She hadn't even known her mother was pregnant.

Gram lifted the jarred pickles out of the hot water bath, and set them aside to watch for the lids to pop. That had been one of Chelsea's jobs as a child. She had watched the jar lids until they sealed, making a soft popping sound, and indenting the lid. She remembered her bare legs sticking to the red vinyl seats of the kitchen chairs because of the heat and humidity built up in the kitchen. She could still taste those pickles. They'd always open a jar for dinner the day they made them and discussed flavors, textures and what they'd do differently next year.

Chelsea leaned on her hand and remembered the good times. There were many. Exhaling a contented breath, she walked over to Gram and gave her big hug. "What can I do to help?" she asked.

Gram started to point to the cooling jars and stopped herself. They smiled at each other, realizing their thoughts had been running in the same direction. A lid popped and the sound made them smile, a reminder of pleasant days gone by, shared with people she loved.

Maybe I just need some time to watch lids pop, Chelsea thought. Chelsea caught Gram's look and knew that she suspected something else was wrong in Chelsea's world. She also knew that Gram would wait and pray and hope that one day Chelsea would be ready to surrender her secret.

A loud banging came from the screen door at the front of the house and a tall man with dark curly hair and a straw hat stood on the other side. He was wearing in bib overalls and holding a metal berry bucket.

"Do I know you?" Chelsea asked, her eyes dancing with laughter at the sight of the normally dapper engineer.

"Are you mocking me, young lady?" Dane asked, an eyebrow rose in insincere warning. Reaching for the door handle, he let himself in.

Chelsea, recognizing that look, giggled and scurried across the living room and through the swinging kitchen door before he could catch her. Pretending nonchalance, she crossed the kitchen and hid behind her Grandmother.

She heard long strides across the living room and the metal berry bucket clanking as the kitchen door swung open to reveal Dane with a predatory grin on his face. He stopped short when he saw Gram, her arms crossed, a glint of humor in her eyes. "What do we have here?" she asked motioning toward the bucket and the overalls.

Chelsea peeked over Gram's shoulder. She could see Dane's look that said, you may be safe now, but wait till I get you alone.

Dane heard a snort and saw Grandpa Pete leaning against the doorway of the back porch, taking off his muddy boots. "'Pears to me there's some berries that need picked," he said, making his way into the steamy kitchen and heading toward the coffee pot. "Care for a cup?" he asked Dane, ignoring the look his granddaughter gave him as she slowly came out of hiding.

"Actually," Dane said, smiling at the older man and casting a look at the now curious Chelsea, "I was heading over to the old Bennett place this morning to pick the last of the raspberries." The Ross's had won the picking rights to the old Bennett place at last year's Harvest of Talents. Dane hadn't been home many times in the past year, but when he was, he and his father had picked raspberries and handed them out to their neighbors and friends.

"Who won the berry bucket rights this year?" Gram asked.

Chelsea realized that her problem at the Harvest of Talents had probably kept her grandmother from even entering.

"Well, actually," Dane said, holding out the tin pail and leaning towards Gram, "I'm here to pass the pail."

Gram looked confused as Grandpa filled in the blanks. "I knew you had forgotten to put your name in, so I put it in at the last minute, and you won," Grandpa said, looking pleased with himself.

Gram looked from Grandpa to Dane and back again. Chelsea knew she had prayed for the berry picking rights to the Bennett place for years. Gram grabbed the bucket and did a little dance around the kitchen, her cheeks, already pink from the heat in the kitchen turned rosy. Grandpa beamed at her obvious delight and took her hand and did a turn, spinning her under his upraised arm. She stopped, slightly off out of breath and grinning, planted a kiss on his cheek. She leaned over to Dane and gave him one too. "Thank you, young man."

Dane looked at Chelsea and winked. She smiled a grateful smile, thinking it was thoughtful of him to bring the good news himself. Besides, she was finding she enjoyed being around him.

"What about it?" Grandpa asked.

"What about what, Grandpa?"

"What about the berry picking and official passing of the pail. Looks like this last batch of berries belongs to both the Ross's and the Livingston's. Maybe you'd better go watch this Ross fellow and make sure he doesn't take more'n his share."

Caught up in the excitement of the moment, Chelsea said yes before thinking. She threw her Grandpa a good natured frown at his obvious attempt to get her out of the house, but decided it might be just the thing she needed. "What about the pickles, Gram? Don't you need my help?"

"I think the lids will pop all by themselves this year," she said, smiling good-naturedly. "Sometimes you just have to let things cool for a while, and it all works out."

Enigmatic, Chelsea thought, casting a glance between her grandmother and the still smiling Dane. She could have sworn a look passed between them. Downright enigmatic. Chelsea made her decision, aided by her mouth-watering at the thought of fresh red raspberries, and went to change her clothes and get her camera.

"Wear long sleeves," she heard Dane call after her as she ran up the stairs to change.

Chelsea rolled her eyes and went to find an old flannel shirt. She'd take her blue jean jacket too. She put on an old seed corn cap and pulled her pony tail through the hole in the back and took the stairs two at a time as she went back downstairs to meet the waiting Dane. She grabbed a pair of leather gloves from the storage box at the bottom of the coat rack.

She looked ready, Dane thought, checking out her berry picking outfit. Cute and sweet too, he thought. Aware of where his thoughts were going, Dane opened the door and walked to the pickup. He opened Chelsea's door and closed it after her as she slid in.

"Have fun," Grandpa called as they drove away. "And don't eat more'n you bring home!"

Chelsea settled back against the seat of the old pickup truck, her antennae suddenly going up. She was alone with a man besides Grandpa for the first time in a long time. She thought about that. She wasn't uncomfortable, but a little wary.

Dane could see that Chelsea's body was tense, but determined that he would give her absolutely no reason to do anything but enjoy her day. He looked at her as the pail sat between them on the dusty vinyl seat. Did she know how pretty she looked? Did she know that she also carried a slightly haunted look on her face wherever she went? He shifted his eyes back on the road just as she turned to look at him. Her wary smile told him she was determined to enjoy the day. He wished they'd packed a lunch, but a few hours of berry picking would have to be enough. He was looking forward to spending time with her, probing a little, finding out what caused that haunted look, and if he could possibly help her.

Chelsea rolled down the window of the pickup and tried to concentrate on the flowering weeds and prairie flowers that lined the ditches on either side of the road. As the seasons changed, they would be covered in shimmering ice and then powdered with a thick layer of snow during the winter months. She took a deep breath and settled back into the seat. Just a drive with a friend. She took an inventory of her secret, and boxed it up tightly. No one was going to make her open that box. Feeling it securely tucked away, Chelsea began to make small talk. They talked about his father and the fall planting season and laughed over the antics of a squirrel doing a dance on the high wires above the dirt road. How the little acrobats hung on as they ran and jumped across the wires, Chelsea didn't know.

They reached the Bennett place and turned in the drive, kicking up a cloud of white dust behind them. Dane grabbed the berry pail and came around to help Chelsea out of the truck. They side yard of the old Bennett place was filled with a mass of prickly raspberry vines. Dane, thankful for the leather gloves, held back the brambles while Chelsea began picking the ripe berries. They worked well as a team, and Chelsea began to enjoy the fresh air and bright sunshine. She began humming as they filled the pail with red, ripe berries, proving her grandfather right as Dane ate more than he picked. Occasionally Chelsea stopped to pick up her camera and snap a few pictures. One she particularly liked was a close up of a branch with delicate white blooms, rich red berries, and the pointed thorns that protected the vines.

As the sun climbed higher in the sky, Dane began to feel frustrated. He was certainly happy that Chelsea was enjoying herself, but they had been picking for nearly two hours, and he had gotten no closer to Chelsea's secrets than he had been when they started.

With fingers stained with raspberry juice and faces flushed from the sun, they arrived back at the Livingston's by noon and handed the pail full of pure berry goodness to a delighted Gram.

"You wait right here while I bring you your share," Sharon said to Dane as she moved through the kitchen door, obviously delighted with the morning's efforts.

"Just keep them," he said, following her into the kitchen and shaking his head as she offered him half. "But if you should happen to have an extra jar or two of raspberry jelly that you needed to get rid of, I'm sure Pops wouldn't mind."

"Of course I will," she said, putting a hand on his arm and leading him back into the dining room. "And thank you for getting Chelsea out of the house this morning. She hasn't left the farm much, unless it's alone, to take pictures."

"I'd like to be her friend," Dane said, walking with her toward the front door.

"She needs that right now, Dane. But nothing more." Dane saw her pause, as if she was thinking how much to share. She looked up and studied him for a moment. "Her heart is fractured. I don't think it's just about the attack."

Dane felt like his own suspicions had been confirmed. She made him consider his own motives. Was he attracted to Chelsea in a way he shouldn't be or did he care about her because he sensed her suffering? It was something he needed to pray about. He stood at the screen door and watched as Chelsea sat talking to Gramps as she pulled burrs off of her pant legs and shoestrings. Maybe he'd better back off. Maybe she was just fine, and he was imagining the whole thing. Maybe it would be better for both of them if he withdrew until he knew what he wanted. Was he trying to help her, or were his motives more selfish?

They said their goodbyes, and Chelsea and her grandparents went inside to share a lunch of tuna fish sandwiches, chips, pickles and fresh berries and cream. When the dishwasher was loaded, Chelsea climbed the stairs to her room sat on her bed and picked up the present she had made for Jeanine's shower. It was arrangement of photos of Jeanine and her brother and sisters. She had arranged the photos into the shape of a tree. A family tree. In the center of the collage was a photo of one of the Renault's famous English walnut trees in full color, surrounded by the photos of Jeanine's generation. There was an empty spot, now decorated with a pink foot print that Chelsea hoped would soon be filled with a picture of the newest little Renault. The whole thing was matted in forest green. She had used her calligraphy skills to write 'Renault Family Tree' at the top. Satisfied, she finished wrapping the shower gift and added a large pink bow. It wasn't your usual shower gift, but she knew Jeanine would like it. She had a few hours before the shower, and decided to work on her plans for the future. She had been praying about some things, and she needed to put some numbers to them. She spent the rest of the day in her room at her computer, working out the details of her plan. Once she set the plan into motion, there'd be no going back. That was fine with her. She was more than ready for a change.

Chapter Eleven

Dane was back at the church, setting up for the next youth group meeting when Josh's mom came in. This time her eyes were shimmering with tears, but she had an excited smile on her face.

"I saw your truck when I drove by the church, and knew you'd want to know," she said standing near to him as he set up another folding chair. You won't believe the change in Josh since he started going to your youth group. He's like a new young man," she said obviously pleased with the outcome. "We'd like to invite you to dinner to celebrate," she said looking up at him, her face alive with excitement.

He didn't usually do that sort of thing. That was more Pastor Green's territory. He didn't want to see Lisa's excitement about what was going on in Josh's life diminish, but he also didn't want to have the whole town thinking there was something going on between them.

"Tell you what," he said, searching for a compromise. "Why don't we meet at the Ice Cream Caboose and have a celebratory ice cream cone? I'd like the chance to talk to Josh about some opportunities coming up in youth group, and we may need your input. Some of it may involve traveling, and I wanted to make sure we had your approval.

Lisa was fine with the idea of meeting at the Caboose, as the locals called it. They coordinated their plans to meet at seven on Thursday night. It shouldn't be too crowded on a Thursday night, Dane thought. If people saw them, especially with Josh there, they wouldn't mistake it for more than it was. A simple meeting between youth group leader and one of his youth group parents.

Chelsea arrived at the shower right on time and entered the front door into a sea of pink decorations. Pink streamers hung from the ceiling, an arrangement of pink roses decorated the gift table and bunches of pink and white balloons floated in the corners of the room. Some even hung from the ceiling fan. Chelsea was sure that was Lisbeth's doing. The Renault family had turned out in force, and the room was filled with chattering relatives.

"We're so glad you're here, Chelsea," Lisbeth's mother said when she spotted Chelsea in the doorway. "Take a seat anywhere. I've got to go stir the punch." Chelsea spotted the gift table and set her package down on the already full table. She turned to find a seat, only to bump into the only son of the family. He looked incredibly out of place in the sea of pink. It almost made her laugh.

Chelsea felt a hand on her arm and someone stepped gently in front of her.

"What are you doing here, bro?" Lisbeth said. "Girls only. Out with you," she said, playfully shoving her older, much stronger brother toward the front door.

"But . . ." was all he managed to get out before she closed the door behind him.

"Guess I took care of him, didn't I?" Lisbeth said, putting a protective arm around Chelsea's shoulders, guiding her to a chair and sitting down next to her. The cake was cut and consumed and the presents were opened. Jeanine held up the photo collage Chelsea had made and it drew admiring 'oohs and 'aahs from the family. They played a game with diaper pins and Chelsea, not wanting to draw attention to herself, tried to lose. Unfortunately, it wasn't so much skill as chance and she won the game, giving her the opportunity to pick a prize from the white wicker basket on the gift table. The game winners had been opening their gifts and giving them to the mother-to-be. Chelsea carefully un-wrapped the gift she had chosen and found a pair of hand-knit baby booties. As her fingers touched the soft yarn and shiny ribbons tied in delicate bows, tears began to fall. She wasn't expecting them and she couldn't contain them. She crossed the room before they got out of control and handed the present to Jeanine. She made a run for the bathroom, trying to stem the tide until she was someplace safe. As she headed up the stairs, she ran into David coming down. He hadn't left the house after all. She couldn't let him see her like this. She turned and fled, out the kitchen door and down the back steps. It wasn't long before she heard footsteps behind her and quickened her pace, trying to outrun whoever it was to the Livingston property line and home.

She knew she owed whoever it was an explanation, but she wasn't ready to go into it now. She wasn't sure she ever would be. She whirled around as she felt a hand on her shoulder, half expecting to see David. Instead it was Lisbeth, a look of concern on her face.

"What's the matter, Chelsea? You look like you've seen a ghost."

That's all it took. The dam holding back her tears broke and she sat on the ground in a bundled heap. Lisbeth dropped down beside her and wrapped an arm around her shoulders, concern etched on her face. Chelsea's tears eventually ran their course as Lisbeth sat patiently, waiting for an explanation of her best friend's distress.

"I'm sorry, Chelsea said, wiping her nose on the last of the tissues from her pocket. "I thought I could do that."

"Nothing to be sorry for Chelsea. After what you've been through, you're doing great. I should have thought that all this noise and confusion might be difficult for you. I'm sorry."

Chelsea looked at her friend and realized she couldn't tell her the real reason for her tears. "I've just been a little emotional lately," she said instead.

"Understandable," Lisbeth said waiting while Chelsea collected the spent tissues from the ground and stood up, straightening her clothes. "If there's anything I can do, Chelsea," her friend said, "let me know."

Chelsea smiled and patted her friend's hand. "You've done enough, Lisbeth. Thank you. I hope I didn't ruin the shower."

"No harm done, Chelsea. You know the Renaults. They're generally loud enough that you wouldn't hear a cannon go off in the next room."

Chelsea smiled and hugged her best friend. They walked a few steps toward her grandparent's house.

She was thankful for a friend who was ready to leave her own sister's baby shower to watch over her. "No, you go back inside, Lisbeth. I'm fine now. It usually comes like a flood and leaves the same way."

After reassuring her friend one more time, Chelsea brushed her hair out of her eyes and headed down the path through the acres of trees between the two farms. She hadn't gone twenty steps when she found she wasn't alone.

"Wait," a voice said from behind her on the path.

Chelsea nearly jumped out of her skin as her adrenaline spiked and she fought the impulse to run. She was home and safe. She took a deep breath and turned around. This time it was David. His voice had dropped an octave since she her junior class prom and he had filled out. He looked like he worked out regularly in a gym. Gone were the nerdy computer whiz glasses that had hidden the Renault hazel eyes. She stirred herself from her musings and wondered what he was doing out here. She stood there, arms wrapped around middle, waiting for him to tell her what he wanted. She really wasn't in the mood to rehash their relationship.

He seemed to sense her need to process, because he stayed quiet for a moment, waiting for her thoughts to settle down.

That type of sensitivity was not at all like the David she used to know, Chelsea thought. The old David had been completely self-absorbed and all his conversations had centered on himself.

She let her hands fall by her side and he came to walk beside her as she began walking slowly down the path toward the Livingston's farm. Their arms would bump occasionally, bringing back memories of the many trips they had made down this path that separated the two families' farms. They hadn't walked far when he put a hand on her arm and stopped her.

"Chelsea, I'm sorry I was such an idiot. What I did to you prom night was terrible. I'm sorry I ruined a special day for you."

Chelsea merely nodded her forgiveness, and began to walk on.

"There's something I need to tell you about that night and the years since I went away."

Chelsea stopped and turned to face him and waited while he seemed to be choosing his words carefully. He looked different, she thought. Gone was the crazed computer whiz kid look. It had been replaced by a peace Chelsea had never seen in him before.

"I have a confession to make Chelsea. I'm an alcoholic. I have been since high school."

Chelsea closed her eyes and an involuntary groan escaped. She should have known. She should have seen the signs. If she had, she could have helped. Instead, she had spent her last year of high school hating him for what he had done. She had never considered that he'd had a real problem.

"I was drunk the night of the prom, and for most of the next three years. I joined a Christian drug rehab program and got straight about six months ago. I've wanted to apologize, but this was my first chance."

"Do your sisters know about this?" Chelsea asked. Certainly Lisbeth would have told her something if she had known.

"Only mom and dad. I told them when I finally hit rock bottom, and they helped me get into the program. I'm trying to make amends to the people I'd hurt, a few at a time. You were one of the first. I treated you badly, and I'm sorry."

What could she say? Of course she forgave him. She took a few seconds to digest the information, and then gave him a big hug. Chelsea could feel the walls come down between them and she was glad to have her friend back.

David looked down at the ground and hesitated, digging a toe into the loose dirt on the path. "I was wondering if there was still a chance, between us Chelsea. You were the best thing I had going for me." He looked into her eyes and waited for her answer.

"You know I'll always care about you David, but not in that way," she said, laying a hand on her arm. "I'm sorry I wasn't there for you when you needed me. I never would have guessed you were struggling. You seemed so happy and confident when you came home."

"All false courage, Chelsea. Straight from a bottle."

She could see that his apology was heartfelt and gave him a reassuring hug. "If I can do anything for you David, let me know," she said, echoing her best friend's words a few moments ago. She waited to see if there was more he needed to say, but the moment seemed over, so she said her goodbyes and headed down the path toward home. Restoration was the word that came to mind. Another piece of her life fell back into place. It felt good to have David back in her life, too.

Chapter Twelve

Dane pulled up to the Caboose in time to see Lisa and Josh open the front door and go into the ice cream shop ahead of him. He opened the door to the truck and stepped out on the sidewalk. As soon as his foot hit the sidewalk, he felt an unsettling in his heart. "Why am I feeling uncomfortable about this, Lord?" he prayed as he walked into the old fashioned ice cream parlor's front door. Josh waved him over and he took a seat beside the young man in a booth along the wall. He nodded toward Lisa and smiled at the hope that he saw on her face.

"I love this place," Josh said, looking around at the railroad memorabilia on the walls. There were railroad crossing signs, and signed photographs of famous entertainers and politicians that had traveled in that very train car. Even old train tickets and a blue felt conductor's hat decorated the wall above their booth.

"Did you know," Josh asked, "that early settlers rode the train for half price tickets if they were coming to Kansas to buy land. If they did by land, their ticket price went toward the sale of the land?"

Dane was impressed by his knowledge of the history of Kansas railroads, and knew that sometimes, if you could find something a kid was passionate about, you could steer them in the right direction. Dane had a good friend who taught history courses at the university. Maybe he could arrange for the three of them to spend the day together.

"The railroad still hauls a huge amount of the grain from around here to the coasts where it's shipped overseas," Josh said with an enthusiasm that Dane hadn't seen before.

Dane looked around at the old railroad dining car and remembered his father telling him that the booth's padded leather seats were original to the dining car, which was in use in the early 1900's. Jerry, the owner of the ice cream shop had found it in a junk yard and restored it to original condition. It had been a labor of love, and the polished wood trim and velvet curtains that used to hold back the heartland's dust looked in mint condition.

Dane's attention was brought back to the present as the waitress came for their order. She was a Renault, Dane thought. One of the middle daughters, he guessed. Her nametag said Connie. He would have to ask Pastor Ben if one of the Renault's girls worked at the Caboose.

"It's on me, Josh," Dane said, "so fire away."

Josh ordered a banana split with extra chocolate topping, and Lisa ordered a single scoop chocolate cone with sprinkles. Dane decided on a hot fudge sundae as Josh gathered the menus and placed them behind the old glass conductor's lantern that held the menus against the Caboose's rich red and gold patterned walls. Dane, still felt slightly unsettled, and was ready to get down to the business. They had a lot to talk about if his plans for the rest of Josh's summer were going to become a reality.

"Mom said you had something you wanted to talk to me about," Josh said, sipping the cold water from the frosty glass the waitress had brought to the table.

"How would you like to be a camp counselor in couple of weeks? I'm going to be the camp leader, and I could use another good counselor. You'd earn a little spending money, and you'll be able to use the camp facilities when you're off duty."

"Yes," Josh said as he did a fist pump in the air. "I'd love it." He looked at his mom to make sure she approved and was rewarded with a smile and a nod.

"What will he need to take with him?" Lisa asked, seeming a little hesitant now that she had given her okay.

Dane knew that money was tight for the small family and assured her that all Josh needed was several changes of casual clothes and a swimming suit. He could tell by looking at her face that the idea was growing on her. He wondered how long it had been since she'd had any quality time to herself. He started to wonder what a young single mom would do with her free time and stopped himself. What she did in her free time was none of his business. Chelsea Livingston's face flashed before his eyes and a thought rolled thought his mind. He wondered where she was as this very moment. Did she have someone she could depend on? As far as he could tell, there was no boyfriend back in St. Louis. He didn't know why that thought made him so happy. He remembered her blonde ponytail bobbing as they had talked, her blue eyes sparkling as they had filled the berry pail, occasionally catching one in his mouth that she tossed in the air. His heart warmed as he thought about her. He wondered if she felt the same thing.

Dane's thought were interrupted as Josh asked for details of the camp. He gladly provided them and even pulled a brochure out of his pocket with a web site address so they could look up any information they needed. Dane finished his ice cream and got ready to leave. He guessed the unsettled feeling earlier had been his imagination. He grabbed the check over Lisa's objections and started to get up from the table. He heard the bell over the ice cream shop's door ring and looked up to see the object of his earlier imaginings framed in the doorway.

Dane Ross is here with another woman, Chelsea thought, stopping involuntarily in her tracks. She clamped a lid on her traitorous emotions and walked to the counter to pick up the quart of ice cream her grandparents had ordered. Dane could sit with whoever he wanted to, Chelsea thought. It was no business of hers. She paid for the ice cream and headed for the door, emotions firmly check, opened her card door and settled into the driver's seat. As she reached down to put the key into the ignition, she heard a firm knock on her window. It was Dane. He must be done with his date already, she thought. He motioned for her to roll down her window. She pushed the button that lowered the window and chanced another look at the handsome man. None of that Chelsea, she warned herself. He's obviously taken. She shot him a friendly smile and got a grin in return. They stood there looking at each other for a moment until Chelsea finally spoke. "Did you enjoy your ice cream?" she asked. She thought about asking him if he enjoyed his date, but decided to mind her own business.

Dane was trying to find the words to let her know it wasn't what she might think it was, but didn't know how to bring up the subject. He decided the truth would be best. "I just asked Josh Warner to be a counselor at the Youth Camp I'm directing in August, and we needed his mother's permission." There, that would let her know it wasn't a date. Or did it?

Chelsea hadn't known Dane was so involved in his girlfriend's life. He hadn't mentioned anything about his relationship with Josh Wagner or his mother when they were berry picking.

"That's great," Chelsea said, meaning it. Dane would be a great influence on the teenagers at the church. She didn't know why the knowledge that Dane had a girlfriend stung, but it did. She kept her face impassive and started the car, putting it into gear. She looked up at Dane and then at his hands that were still holding on to her door, she wondered why he wasn't moving. He wasn't even saying anything.

When he realized what he was doing, Dane stepped back from the car. He had been practically crawling inside the low slung vehicle. He ran his hand through his hair as he watched her back out and her drive away. What he wouldn't give to be inside her head right now, for more reasons than one. He went back in the ice cream parlor and paid the check. Josh and Lisa had been waiting and walked back out with him when he was finished.

Lisa put a hand on his arm, her blue eyes searching his. "I want to thank you for the ice cream and for asking Josh to help at camp."

Dane could feel Lisa trembling, and didn't know why. The why suddenly occurred to him as she rose up on tiptoe and kissed his cheek. He could feel his face flush as the Renault girl gave him a look he couldn't quite place as she watched him through the front windows. He looked around to see who else might have noticed, but decided it didn't matter. The only one he cared about had just driven away. He took off his hat and wiped his face with the back of his hand. He wasn't sure how he'd gotten himself in this position, but he knew that he shouldn't counsel the Wagner family anymore. He put in a call to Pastor Green to let him know that he needed to take over their pastoral care. He wasn't interested in Lisa Wagner, but the relationship had just become too complicated to continue. On top of that, he may just have just blown any chance he had with Chelsea. He put his hat back on his head and started the pickup. The drive home was a long one as he tried to figure out what to do about Chelsea. What he wanted to do, and what he probably should do were becoming two very different things.

The next morning, Chelsea got up with a goal in mind. She went downstairs, poured a cup of coffee and went out on the porch to spend a few minutes with her Bible. She needed God's direction for the day. She watched the mist rising off the fields burn away and felt a peace about her plan settle into her heart. The next thing she knew, she was standing in front of the Purchase Community News office. She stood outside the door for a moment, gathering her courage. She heard the familiar sound of a scripture running through her mind.

"*A man's heart plans his way, But the Lord directs his steps.*"

She sent up a silent prayer that He would direct her steps, took a deep breath, and opened the door. She was immediately greeted by the newspaper's friendly receptionist.

Chelsea remembered the young woman from high school. They were close to the same age. She also remembered seeing the smiling, round-faced brunette at church the last time she'd been home for a visit. "Marsha, right?" Chelsea asked, looking for a name plate on the tidy desk, but not seeing one.

"That's right," Marsha said. "Purchase News receptionist and part-time reporter."

Chelsea took a step back when she heard the word reporter.

Marsha pushed back her chair and came around to shake Chelsea's hand.

Chelsea shook hands hesitantly, putting up her mental shields against any invasive questions Marsha might have.

No questions came though, and the receptionist seemed to bubble over with welcome as she motioned for Chelsea to have a seat.

"And you must be Chelsea," she said, looking at the manila envelope in Chelsea's hand. "And this must be what Mr. Frank has been waiting for," she said, taking the envelope from Chelsea's outstretched hand and sitting down in her chair, rolling her ample frame under the desk. "Mind if I take a peek?"

She shook her head. She was curious about what someone actually in the newspaper business would think of her photos. If Marsha was anything like the other reporters Chelsea had run into recently, she knew her photos didn't stand a chance. She prepared herself for the worst.

Marsha carefully pulled out the eight by ten's, and laid each one on her desk until they nearly covered the desktop. "Oh my," she said, a look of awe on her face. "Chelsea, these are beautiful."

Chelsea's face flushed with pleasure. She felt like a mother whose child had just been complimented. That thought sent a shaft of pain through her midsection that caused her to flinch.

"Are you alright?" Marsha asked, a look of concern on her face. "Can I get you a glass of water or a cup of tea?"

"I'm fine," Chelsea said, struggling to keep a look that masked her true feelings in place. The pain passed and Chelsea straightened in her chair and watched as Marsha's attention was drawn back to her photos.

After studying them for another moment, Marsha pointed to one of the photos. "This picture tells a story, Chelsea. In fact, they all do," she said, sweeping her hand over the pictures lying on the desk.

Chelsea was afraid to believe it. She knew she had captured the spirit of giving at the Harvest of Talents, but had wondered if anyone else would be able to see it. She had focused the camera on her grandmother's hands as she had exchanged a pie for money to support the needy in the community. Chelsea had altered the background of the picture so that all that was visible was the actual exchange. It was a picture of the giving and receiving that made up the mosaic of small town life.

"Now I know what Mr. Frank was talking about, Chelsea. You have a gift."

The pleasant words from a reporter, even a part-time one were a nice change from the harsh questions that had been lobbed at her by the defense attorney and reporters in St. Louis in the last few months. They had questioned everything from the way she had been dressed the night of the attack, to why was she in the park

Free to Fly

alone so late at night. Chelsea had been warned that it would be like that, but the questions still stuck like barbs in her soul.

"He's away from the office right now," Marsha said, interrupting Chelsea's thought process, "but if you want to leave these with me, I'll make sure he gets them."

Chelsea was flooded with feelings of pleasure as she realized she may have made a sale on her first try. She shook Marsha's hand, and left the newspaper office feeling lighter than she had in a while. She stopped long enough to pick up a few things that Gram had wanted from the grocery store and drove home, dreaming of hanging out a shingle--Chelsea Livingston Photography. Her only hesitancy was working for a newspaper. After her earlier experience with reporters, she wasn't sure she wanted to work that closely with one. Even a bubbly one from Purchase, Kansas.

On her drive home, she thought about the one of the photos she had held back. It was the photo of the beautiful white blooms, the full ripe fruit, and thorns of the raspberry bush. When she had pulled it out if its envelope, she had instantly seen a picture of her life with God. There were the times when her life was full of promise and blooming. And then there were the times when she felt she was being fruitful. Times when she went to help a neighbor, or prayed for someone in need. Then there were times like she had felt most recently, when she felt the thorns that the world had to offer when she got too far removed from her place on the vine.

She had realized that morning picking berries that God had not caused the pain in her life, but in His infinite wisdom was turning even the thorns for her good. Feeling more hope than she had for a while, Chelsea parked the SUV in the barn, and carried in the groceries.

"Is that you, Chelsea?" Gram asked, taking a tray of cookies out of the oven.

Chelsea pushed open the kitchen door and set the sacks of groceries on the counter.

Gram slid hot chocolate chip oatmeal cookies off the tray onto a rooster shaped plate waved the plate under Chelsea's nose. "Mmm," Chelsea said as she put the groceries away. She hummed as she rinsed her hands and then sat down at the kitchen table and picked up a warm cookie.

"Someone seems happy this afternoon," looking at her granddaughter, a question in her eyes. "Good news at the newspaper?" she asked, rolling more cookie dough into small balls and placing them on the cookie sheet.

Chelsea heard the back door slam, and her grandfather walked into the kitchen testing the air with an exaggerated sniffing sound. "What smells so good in here?"

"Chelsea was just going to give me some good news, dear. Come and have a cookie," she said, handing the older man a plate and a napkin. "I think your grandfather can smell cookies from several counties away," Gram said, smiling at her husband of fifty-five years. "Let's see, fifty-five years, times fifty-two weeks, times two dozen cookies. That's over sixty thousand cookies I've made him over all those years. And they're all his favorite."

"Chocolate chip, my favorite," Gramps said, holding up a cookie and winking at Chelsea.

"See what I mean?"

Gram rolled their eyes as her grandfather walked over and gave his wife a kiss on the cheek. "Got to have some milk with those cookies don't we?" he asked, reaching for three glasses and then filling them with cold milk from the refrigerator.

How many times had they sat, just like this, around the old kitchen table and talked about everything and nothing? The moment confirmed in Chelsea's heart that this was where she belonged. Not necessarily at this table, but in this town. She knew her future was in front of her. She just wasn't sure where to start looking.

Gram put the last batch of cookies in the oven and set the egg timer for eight minutes. "I made a batch of freezer jam from those berries you and Dane picked last week," the older woman said, nudging Gramps with her elbow when he dunked a cookie and dribbled milk down his chin. "Kids," she said, reaching for a napkin, unfolding it and tucking it in the front of his shirt. Grandpa beamed, obviously delighted, with the fresh warm cookies and her attention. Chelsea had seen the looks that passed between the marriage partners and best friends. Chelsea dreamed of a relationship like that. To know someone inside out and to still love them, faults and all. Her heart wondered if that would ever be possible for her. She couldn't imagine sharing her secret and having a man love her like that. No holds barred. All in. She sighed and suddenly lost her appetite. It was as if the light in the room had gone out. Grief threatened to overwhelm her. She quietly changed mental gears to concentrate on the conversation going on around her. Gram handed Gramps another napkin and then looked expectantly at Chelsea, waiting to hear her good news.

Chelsea shared her conversation with Marsha at the newspaper and accepted congratulations all around.

"It's not a done deal yet," she warned them, "but it looks hopeful. You could be looking at the next contributor to the Purchase Community News," she said, trying to muster up some of her previous enthusiasm. Feeling suddenly weary, she finished her cookies and went to her room. She needed some time to think.

Chapter Thirteen

Dane hadn't seen Chelsea for nearly a week, but she was never far from his mind. The sadness that clouded her features at the Harvest of Talents haunted him. He had been praying for her regularly, but he had decided not to get emotionally involved. He saw no chance of a relationship now. It was too late. She had practically ignored him on the street the other day. He had tried to tell her he wasn't involved with Lisa Wagner, but he wasn't sure she had gotten the message. She would be going back to St. Louis soon, and he had never been one for long range relationships.

The five weeks of Chelsea's leave had passed quickly, and Chelsea found herself hoping she wouldn't have to return to St. Louis, but she needed a way to make money, and so far, her photography wasn't paying her way. She'd always been one to pay her bills, and if God wanted her to return to St. Louis in order to be able to do it, she would. In the meantime, she spent hours with her camera, taking pictures at local events and scenery in the area around Purchase. She had been asked several times already to do a wedding and even a set of senior pictures. Maybe she could come back to Purchase on the weekends and build a photography business of her own. An idea was forming in the back of her mind, but she was almost afraid to take it out and look at it. She had asked God to confirm it if it was His will. She found photography both relaxing and exciting. She was excited every time she got proofs back from the developers, wondering if any of them would be special. Her cell phone rang and she flipped it open and held it to her ear. Was this God, answering her prayer?

"Chelsea, I'm glad I caught you. This is Marsha at the News. I just talked to Mr. Frank, and he wants to run two more of your pictures this week and two next week. That's nine pictures this month already. He's been getting a lot of positive feedback from his readers," her new friend added.

Chelsea took a minute to absorb the news. She thanked Marsha, held her phone close to her chest and did a little dance in the living room. She sent up a silent prayer of thanks for the favor she'd found with Mr. Frank.

"Mr. Frank said he'll need you to come sign a contract stating you are the sole owner of the photos now that you're a regular contributor, and the agreed upon amount of payment. He would also like you to stop in and see him. I think he'd really like to hire you on permanently, Chelsea, but he understands that you that you want to go back to your old job. The Purchase Community News could never hope to compete with the money or benefits you were making there."

Chelsea thanked Marsha for the good news, finished the call and then put down her phone. Tears came as Chelsea felt God's purpose in the call. She wanted one more confirmation from His word, and if what she had in mind was God's will, he'd be faithful to lead her. She went to get her purse, and let her Grandmother know where she was going into town to run some errands.

Chelsea settled into her sleek sports car and looked at custom interior with its fully loaded bells and whistles. It all seemed foreign to her now. She had needed an expensive car when she was on the road all the time, but it seemed out of place on the dirt covered back roads she'd been traveling. She opened the windows of the car and let the road dust settle on the immaculate leather interior. She felt as if everything in her life was clicking back into place, as if she'd been off visiting a foreign country and now she was coming home.

Dane saw Chelsea drive by as he was going to the Livingston's to pick up several jars of the raspberry jam. Either she had just ignored him or didn't see him because she didn't even wave. Blonde hair flying and a smile on her face, she looked like a different person than the one he'd first seen on his father's farm. She still carried a the haunted look in her eyes, but he had seen it a lot less often as she seemed to be coming to grips with whatever had put it there in the first place. He was truly happy about that. He might not have had the right words to say to her to help her, but maybe his prayers had helped.

He hadn't known what to do since the day at the ice cream parlor. He was attracted to her. He was interested in her as part of the Purchase Community Church family, of course, but with her, it was personal. He knew she wasn't ready for a relationship, so he had lain low. Not pursuing her, but praying for her. He prayed she'd know that she wasn't at fault for the attack, and that God was with her. He prayed that she would find God's perfect path for her life, and that no bitterness or jealousy would overtake her. Bitterness because of what she had suffered, jealousy because so many other people were walking around living their lives, not even aware of how blessed they were.

In the short time that he'd known her, he didn't think it would happen, but his own experience told him it was possible. He had spent some time at college fighting bitterness that he couldn't enjoy his chosen profession-the clergy. He also went through a period of being envious of those clergy who were practicing and didn't seem to be as grateful for the opportunity as they should be. God had dealt quite firmly with him about both, and he could see the wisdom of God's directing his path now, but he certainly didn't want Chelsea to have to deal with those feelings on top of everything else.

What exactly was everything else, he wondered. He still sensed a sorrow in Chelsea that he couldn't put a finger on. He was glad to see her smiling as she passed him on the road, and he wondered what had put that smile on her face. Dane turned his truck around, and followed Chelsea into town. She parked in front of the Purchase News and went inside. She came back out shortly after, a paper in her hand. She began walking down the street toward the diner. He backed out of his parking spot, pulled up beside her.

She surprised him by leaning over and looking into the passenger side of the pickup. "Are you stalking me?" she asked, a twinkle in her eye.

Dane saw no sign of fear in her eyes this time-only a gentle humor.

"I guess I am," he said, grinning, pushing his hat back on his head, he reached over to open the passenger side door so she could get in. "How about lunch?" he asked as she climbed in and shut the door.

"A little early isn't it?" she said, amused, pointing to the clock on the dashboard.

Dane grimaced as he realized it was only 10:30. He was supposed to be at the Livingston's by 11:00 to pick up the jars of raspberry jam. "Actually, I'm supposed to be out at your place."

Chelsea remembered Gram mentioning that Dane would be stopping by that morning. In her rush to sign the contract, she had forgotten all about it. She took one look at the dark hair that curled over his shirt collar. He needed a haircut. He also needed a shave. She had never seen him when he wasn't clean shaven, and the day old growth gave him a kind of dangerous look. She had missed him. "How about celebrating with me instead? It will ruin your lunch, but I feel like a double scoop vanilla sundae with hot fudge and nuts." She considered the calories involved, but her decision was made, it was time to celebrate.

Dane parked the truck and they walked into the Caboose, choosing a booth near the back, Dane watched as Chelsea slid into the padded seat and then took the seat across from her.

"What are we celebrating?" he asked, wanting to reach for her hand but deciding against it.

"We are celebrating the sale of my pictures to the newspaper. Mr. Frank has asked for nine so far, with a promise of more to come."

Dane thought of the package that lay on his dresser. "That's wonderful, Chelsea. You really have an eye for photography. I'd love to see the pictures you took when we were picking berries."

Chelsea glowed under his kind words and settled to the business of ordering her ice cream. She was keeping the possibility of a full-time job to herself. No sense starting rumors if the job didn't pan out, and in Purchase, it didn't take much to start a rumor. They ordered their sundaes and the waitress brought a large glass of ice water for Chelsea and a steaming cup of coffee for Dane. When the sundaes arrived, he alternated sips of hot coffee and large bites of cold ice cream.

"That's a really strange way to eat ice cream," Chelsea said smiling and taking another bite of the hot fudge topping and creamy vanilla ice cream.

"I'll tell you a family secret. My dad is a slurper," Dane said, an eyebrow raised in mock warning.

"Your secret is safe with me," Chelsea said, playing along. "But what exactly is a slurper?"

"When anything was too hot to drink, instead of waiting, he would draw air in with the hot liquid and slurp it. I guess he cooled it enough to be able to enjoy it that way." Dane demonstrated with his hot coffee, and smiled at Chelsea. "My mother thought it was endearing, and he's legendary for the noise he makes." He paused as if remembering. "She used to say that when he was snoring she could sleep better because she knew he was near. What could have driven her crazy was something she actually enjoyed," he said, taking a much quieter sip of coffee. "Odd how what we sometimes think are our faults aren't so bad once we shed a little different light on them. That's what love does. Let's you look at the bad things in a slightly different light."

Chelsea dropped her spoon, looked into his dark brown eyes and wondered what he knew. He couldn't possibly know about the abortion. She had told no one in Purchase, and she didn't intend to. She carefully picked up her spoon, laid it on the saucer of her sundae bowl and folded her hands in her lap.

The haunted look was back on Chelsea's face and Dane wanted to know why. He was frustrated. What was it in her past that showed up like a ghost, and then moved on, leaving a sadness and fragility in its wake? He wanted to shake her and make her tell him. Instead, he bit back the words and stayed quiet. He didn't want to spook her. She would tell him someday. He hoped. Then he remembered she would be leaving soon, and wondered if that someday would ever come.

Chelsea gave him a frail smile and laid her napkin on the table. "Thank you for the sundae," she said, picking up her purse.

He stood as she slid out of the booth. She hesitated for a moment, then gave him a hug that was meant to assure him she was alright. "Thank you for being my friend," she said, meaning every word of it. Holding all her emotions in check, she left the ice cream parlor door and walked to her car.

Dane still felt the impression of her arms around his waist as he stood and watched her go. He felt her heartache and was determined to get to the bottom of it, whether she wanted to share or not.

Chelsea pulled her car through the bank drive-through and cashed her check. She intended to use it to repay Gram and

Grandpa for the food she had eaten and her share of the utilities. When she got home, she got out a plain white envelope, stuck the money inside and laid it on the kitchen table. She'd have a talk with Gram and Gramps to see what they thought about her moving back to Purchase. She hoped they'd be happy, but she needed to make sure before she set her other plans in motion. What she was going to do about the other thing, the one she kept hidden, she didn't know.

Chapter Fourteen

Pops Ross crossed the white gravel driveway and walked over to where Dane was scraping the hardened earth off the blades of their sixteen row plow. Soon they would start pulling the plow through the barren fields, burying the wheat stubble, allowing it to be mixed with the soil to help retain moisture.

"How you doing, Pops?" Dane asked, pausing in his work to check on the older man.

Pops Ross shifted his weight and looked off to the horizon. "I'm doing well, son," he said, pausing and wiping his forehead with the back of his good hand. "That's kind of what I wanted to talk to you about. I was wondering if it was just about time you packed up and went back to that engineering job of yours. They must need you at work, and I'm plenty fine to manage the farm by myself. I can hire a man to do the plowing if I need to. Then we'll see about the planting in September."

His father was trying to get rid of him. He thought about that for a few minutes and decided that was healthy. But what was the rush? "You trying to get rid of me, Pops?" Dane asked.

"It's just that I'm well enough to get on with my own life. You don't need to hover anymore."

Dane hadn't realized he was hovering. He bit back a quick answer and decided to give his dad some space. Maybe there was more going on here than he knew. Had he pushed his father too far? Surely he'd still need someone to drive him to his doctor visits and do the heavier work for a while.

"Anyway, lunch is ready," the older man said, slapping his son on the back.

Dane set the table while Pops served yet another casserole. Seemed like half the population of Purchase had been on Pops' doorstep in the days after the accident, offering to help in one way or another. He and Pops had eaten well these last few weeks. "Whose casserole are we eating today?" Dane asked, taking a bit bite of delicious egg, ham and cheese dish. Dane thought the older man blush as he stumbled for an answer.

"Um, this would be Gracie Seaver's casserole, I think," he said, getting busy with his own plate.

Something about mentioning the young widow's name seemed to have flustered his father. "Haven't we had several of her casseroles lately?" he asked. "And weren't those her brownies we ate last night? As I recall, didn't she come and visit you several times in the hospital?"

Pops face flamed red and he put down his fork. Dane's deep brown eyes sparkled with good humor as he watched his father squirm and then let him off the hook. "Do you have a girlfriend, Dad?" Dane asked, enjoying the older man's discomfort.

Pops Ross put his napkin on the table and tilted his chair back. "I suppose you could say that."

Dane leaned over and slapped his father on the back. "Good for you, Pops. It's about time you got back in the dating game. How long have you been seeing each other?"

"About three months," the older man replied, fingering his napkin. "That's not going to be a problem for you?" he asked, looking at his son with concern in his eyes.

"Heck no, Pops. I think it's great. Here I was thinking you were all alone, and you were whooping it up with another woman." Dane realized how he'd framed that last statement as soon as the words left his mouth. "I didn't mean that Dad. Mom's been gone over three years now. You deserve some happiness."

"Gracie's a good woman," Pop's said finally. Her husband passed a few years ago, and her grown children have all moved away. Before the accident, we were having dinner at the diner once a week or so.

Dane remembered Gracie Seaver as a small woman with a big heart. What he remembered most was that she seemed lighthearted and fun to be around. Dane smiled at the thought of his father having a girlfriend. No wonder he was ready to have his grown son leave. It was time for Pops to have his life back. By the look on Pop's face when he talked about Gracie, this could be something serious. "Gracie seems like a nice lady. I'm glad for you Pops."

Pops could handle all but the most arduous jobs himself, but he'd still needed transportation into town for supplies and doctor's appointments for a while. The more Dane thought and prayed about moving his base of operations to Purchase, the more he was convinced it was the right thing to do. Pop was doing well, but Dane wanted to be there for him during planting and harvest seasons. Not close enough to be underfoot, but close enough to keep an eye on him until he was sure he was completely healed. If he started planning now, he could be moved to Purchase by planting time in September. Planting the red winter wheat was almost a sacred ritual to a wheat farmer, and there's no way Pops would let another man drill his wheat if he could do it himself. Dane could see no downside to moving. He would miss having everything he needed at his fingertips like he did in a larger town, but most of his supplies could be ordered over the internet. The house was too small for two bachelor men, so he'd have to find a place of his own. Luckily, when he had taken the place in Salina, he had opted to rent instead of buy. He'd have to pray about it, but the more he thought about it, the more attractive the option seemed . . . he thought of a girl with hair the color of wheat straw and eyes the color of a Kansas sky. What God had in mind there, he didn't know, but he was willing to wait.

Chapter Fifteen

Chelsea extended her leave by taking several weeks of her vacation time. She was still waiting . . . waiting for whatever God wanted to do next. She continued to take pictures, and had even expanded into writing human interest stories to go with them. She felt more fulfilled than she had in years, and had made the decision to stop by the newspaper office and confide in Marsha that she was interested in the full-time job. Chelsea had felt an instant kinship with the friendly receptionist and they had gotten to know each other well in the short time that she'd been home.

Marsha squealed and came around the desk to give Chelsea a hug when she heard the news that Chelsea was considering Mr. Frank's offer. "I know he was planning to expand the paper into two or three other towns, but didn't feel he had the staff to do it. With you on board, he will!"

Chelsea returned her friend's hug, and felt a quiet inner confidence that this was the direction she should go. It felt like the open door she'd been looking for.

"Mr. Frank's out for a few hours, but he'll be back this afternoon. Why don't you fill out this standard application, and we'll see what other information he needs. But what about your job in St. Louis, Chelsea?"

At the thought of St. Louis, Chelsea's good mood vanished, and her hand dropped to her middle. Her joy dimmed as the memories flashed once again through her mind, leaving their evidence on her face.

Marsha looked at Chelsea and seemed to make a decision. "Chelsea, I'm going to tell you something, and if you don't want to hear it, let me know. When I was twenty-one, and in my senior year at college, and I found out I was pregnant. I was in college on a basketball scholarship, and couldn't have afforded to finish otherwise. When I found out I was pregnant, I made an appointment and had an abortion. I'm telling you this because I'm very familiar with what some women experience after they've had an abortion."

Chelsea looked at Marsha for a long moment and couldn't decide whether or not to deny it. She was not prepared to talk to anyone about this, especially someone who was a comparative stranger. She felt frozen to the floor as thoughts bombarded her mind. *Is this a door you're opening, Lord? Is this who I'm supposed to talk to?* She opened her mouth to say something, but Marsha stopped her.

"I didn't mean to put you on the spot. I wanted you to know that if there's ever anything you need to talk about, I'm available." Marsha picked up the previous conversation where it had left off, as if the sentences in the middle had never happened. "Now what can I do for you today?"

Chelsea had a moment of mental whiplash at the turn of the conversation. Did she really hear what she thought she'd heard? The door to her heart and emotions slammed shut. She handed her latest batch of photos to Marsha and picked up her check. Not knowing what to say, Chelsea thanked Marsha, took her paycheck and walked out the door. She got as far as her car, got in and started the engine. A thousand thoughts went through her mind. Did she have the courage to tell Marsha her secret? Was she the answer to Chelsea's prayers? There was only one way to find out. Chelsea turned off the engine and opened her car door. No more running. She was going to get some help.

Marsha beamed when Chelsea walked back in the door. There was another couple in the office now, but Marsha got up and walked over to Chelsea and handed her a small pink business card. She hugged her and winked and went back to her desk. Chelsea looked at the card. *Lifeline Ministries, helping women who have experienced the trauma of abortion,* with a phone number listed on the bottom. A sense of relief and awe filled Chelsea. Relief that such a group existed, and awe that God would send her to Purchase, Kansas to find it. She held the card tightly in her hand, and determined in her mind to call the number on the card. Soon.

She headed once again for her car. She couldn't believe how things were coming together. A few more hurdles to jump and she was home free. Next she would talk to her grandparents about her decision to move back to Purchase permanently, not looking for their permission, but their wisdom. She drove back to the farm, thinking about the pink card in her purse, and the God who answered all her prayers.

"Are you sure you're not just running away?" Gram asked after Chelsea had shared her news about her decision to move home.

Grandpa ate a fresh oatmeal cookie and offered one to Chelsea as they sat at the kitchen table and discussed the move.

"I'm not." Chelsea replied. "At the very least, I feel like I'm coming home to where I belong." Chelsea knew she meant more than just the physical place of Purchase, but to a new home in her heart. "I feel like I've been walking beside God's will for the last few years instead of in the path He knew would be the best for me. My friend Maggie told me it was like following footprints in the snow. Making sure your feet go where He's gone before and made the way."

Maggie had been right about a lot of things. She had been right about the abortion too. She had very gently said that two wrongs don't make a right. Chelsea knew that Maggie had been praying with all her might that she would change her mind. They had read all the literature together and Chelsea knew, deep down in her heart that this wasn't the way to go, but the people at the clinic assured her that it was only a piece of tissue. A fetal mass they called it. They didn't ever really explain what the procedure was or if she would suffer any ill effects.

Chelsea looked up to see Gram and Grandpa exchange a look that said that she had communicated more than she had intended. Chelsea wasn't ready to share her past with anyone, and she hoped that the damage she had inflicted in the past two months hadn't shown on her face. She couldn't tell the ones she loved about the abortion. What if they totally rejected her? Chills ran down Chelsea's spine as the thought of being emotionally separated from her grandparents ran through her mind. She was also ashamed of how judgmental she had been toward others who had been in her situation in the past. No one really knows what's in someone's heart until you walk a mile in their shoes. She knew her grandparents loved her, but she wasn't willing to risk alienating them. A sense of her aloneness with her secret swept over her.

In her heart, she turned toward God, the One that would never leave her and felt the familiar peace of His love cover her heart like a warm blanket. When she had walked back toward Him, asked Him to forgive her for the terrible mistakes she'd made, the God of all comfort had come in and overwhelmed her with His love and acceptance. She knew that she could never be taken out of His hand. Back in those days, she hadn't known what she knew now. That she was forgiven, and the past was wiped away. She was starting again with a clean slate. She pulled her robe of righteousness closely around her shoulders and thanked God again for his patience and loving kindness.

"When my father and mother forsake me, Then the Lord will take care of me . . ."

The scripture ran like a clear, pure stream through her mind. Even if her grandparents rejected her, she'd never be alone.

"I can take the old truck up and get a few loads this weekend," Gramps said. Obviously, plans were already in the works to move their granddaughter home.

Gram reached for a notepad, and started writing down things to be done. Now that the decision had been made, Chelsea could tell they were excited to have their only granddaughter coming home. "I'll get the spare bedroom cleaned out, and we can set up a place for 'yer pictures," Gramps said, an eager look on his face.

"Wait," Chelsea said, holding up both hands. "I have several things I need to take care of before making any kind of move. I have six months of severance coming and some vacation time, so we don't have to make any sudden moves." Chelsea was amused at the speed with which her grandparents had taken over her near future, but even though it was in a loving, caring way, it confirmed in her mind that she needed a place of her own.

She had been quietly looking at houses for rent, and had found a small cottage a block off Main Street and within walking distance of the newspaper. The rent was cheap because of its size, but it had a small front yard that she could fill with flowers and her back yard opened into the city park. She had felt a sense of peace settle over her when she called about it and walked over to look at it earlier in the week. She had said nothing, wanting to make sure it was God's will before she said anything to anyone.

Dane stopped at the implement dealership to pick up a part for the tractor that Pops had ordered. The coffee drinkers were out in force today, filling the small waiting room and discussing everything from politics to the ongoing trash collection crisis in Purchase. Dane had been giving the trash problem some thought, and had even talked to a few people on the city council. The president of the council was retiring soon and was going to spend six months of the year in Florida. Several of the remaining board members had encouraged Dane to run for election to fill his spot.

"I'm telling ya, I've lived in this town sixty years and I'm not about to start paying for someone to carry away my garbage now," a voice said, carrying above several others in the heated discussion.

Finally, a voice of reason sounded above all the others. "If the route was computerized, it would only take half a day to do the entire town. Taxes wouldn't have to go up much at all."

At the mention of taxes going up, the idea was soundly defeated by a number of groans.

Dane liked the idea himself, and wondered who the forward thinking person was who had thought of it. He crossed the room to get to the parts counter and saw a man close to his age, with a muscular build and close cropped blonde hair. The man was obviously familiar with Purchase, but Dane had never seen him before. He looked a lot like Connie Renault. A light went on as Dane realized that this must be the missing Renault brother Pops had told him about. Pops had also told him that David Renault had dated Chelsea for several years in high school. How Pops knew these things, Dane didn't know. He did know that Pops favored Chelsea, and was getting pretty obvious with his hints. He thought Dane was moving a little too slowly in that respect. Dane in fact was moving slowly, but only because he felt it was best for Chelsea. He took one more look at the computer genius who was rapidly gaining support for his idea, paid for his part, and left the dealership. Had David Renault returned to strike up his former relationship with Chelsea? Dane felt a surge of what he could only identify as jealousy. He realized he was being ridiculous. High school was a long time ago. Certainly they had both moved on. He planted his hat on his head, walked to the truck and slammed the door with a little more force than necessary. He headed back to the farm lost in thought. He needed to concentrate on the day ahead. Pops needed the part on the tractor so he could start to move grain.

This time, Dane was going to be there in case the auger jammed. One farm injury was enough.

Chelsea felt good about her move after talking to her grandparents. Then she did the thing she knew in her heart she needed to do the most. She took out the little pink card and went upstairs and made the call. She was nervous, but having prayed about it, felt this was what the Lord was leading her to do. The what-if's had just started to run though her mind when a pleasant voice answered the phone on the other end.

"Lifeline Ministries, how can I help you?"

Chelsea very nearly put the phone back down, but her heartache won out over her fear. Fear of rejection, fear of failure, even a little fear of the unknown. "Hi, I'm interested in finding out what services you provide," Chelsea managed to force out through her tightly pressed lips. Half of her still wanted to keep her secret. The other half couldn't wait to get the pressure off her heart.

"We meet once a week, and a new class starts every eight weeks. We'll be starting a new class on Friday night, and would love to have you sit in if you'd like. Everything is confidential, and we use first names only," the kind voice said. Chelsea looked at the address on the business card. It was in Bentonville, a large city several miles down the road from Purchase. Chelsea was delighted that she would be able to talk about the things that were bothering her and still remain anonymous. She sent up a prayer of thanksgiving and added her name to the list of attendees for next Friday's meeting.

Chapter Sixteen

Dane searched the internet for places for sale in Purchase and found one he liked just north of town. He wasn't ready to talk to a realtor yet. He loved the people of Purchase, but the news would be all over the county by noon. He'd talked to his partner at the engineering business, and neither one could see a problem with Dane working remotely. Dane could drive to Salina once or twice a week to keep on top of new projects, but other than that, he was free to work wherever he wanted. He had told his father his plans, and after a long look, his father had only nodded . . .

"You're not doing this for me, are you son?" his father asked, looking at his arm, still in a sling. "I'm not as laid up as I used to be."

Dane looked at his Father and tried to explain. "Look, Pops. Even when you're well, you can still use a little help with the plowing and planting. I enjoy being in the fields, and would like to be the one to help. But if I'm butting in where I don't belong, I want you to just say so."

Dane felt, more than saw his father relax and wondered what had been going through the older man's mind. He certainly didn't want his father thinking he was moving back to take care of him. At 62, his father was perfectly able to take care of himself, and if Dane had anything to do with it, would stay that way for a long time.

Pops sat down and rested his sore shoulder against the back of the hardwood chair.

"What's on your mind then, son?"

Dane pulled out the chair across from Pops turned it around and sat down, facing the older man. "I can do what I do anywhere, Pops. With the accident, and coming home, I realized how much I like the small town atmosphere and sense of community. I'd like to help the town grow in the right way. We also need to be open to change. We need to keep up with technology, and have a master plan for growth. One of the city council members asked me if I'd be interested in running. I was more excited about that than anything I've done for a long time. It just seems like the time is right. For a lot of reasons," he said cryptically.

Pops nodded and drummed his fingers slowly on the table. "Wouldn't have anything to do with a certain young lady would it?" he said, a grin spreading slowly over his face. "You know son, since your mom died, I haven't always been able to give you good advice, especially about matters of the heart. But I have to say, I do like that young lady."

Dane held up both hands as if to stop the locomotive train of thoughts that just came down the tracks of his father's mind. If he was honest with himself, could that be some of his motivation in moving home? He shook his head and leaned toward his father. "She's leaving Pops. Back to her job in St. Louis." In his heart, he'd had to face reality. As much as he wanted to be the one that helped to erase the haunted look from Chelsea's eyes, it must not be part

Free to Fly

of God's plan. Long distance relationships rarely worked, and she deserved better than that. She deserved the best.

"Just a thought," Pops said as he got up from his chair and pushed it under the table, "but you could do worse than that little girl," he said, taking his dishes and walking toward the kitchen.

Dane honestly didn't know what to say. He just couldn't see any future in it. Chelsea was going back to St. Louis soon, and he also knew she had some other issue that needed to be settled before she could move on with her life. The rape meant nothing to him. He admired her strength and will to survive. He hoped she would continue to fight for healing on the inside. He wanted to help, if she'd let him.

Chelsea settled into her car for the drive to Bentonville. She walked into the one story, non-denominational church and felt instantly at home. There were overstuffed chairs and coffee tables arranged in a group setting. Pillows and thick rugs added to the comfort of the room. The lighting was soft and there was worship music playing in the background. A table with coffee, water and juice was just off to one side.

Marsha greeted Chelsea with a hug and began to introduce her to several other women standing around the drink table, using only their first names. Chelsea felt herself relax, and although she wasn't really planning to participate, when they were all seated she sat forward in her chair, eager to hear what the others had to say.

Marsha opened with prayer. "Father, thank you for these ladies that you have brought here tonight. Thank you for their courage and for your great love for them."

They played a worship song, and as Chelsea sang, she felt her heart open up to what God wanted to do. She would see this thing through. She knew she needed to. All in, as Grandpa used to say. She knew it wasn't going to be easy, revisiting her feelings and reliving her decision to have an abortion, but she trusted Marsha and knew that God had brought her to this place.

By the time the meeting ended, she had cried and laughed and felt God's sweet peace flow into her heart as she relinquished her sin to Him one final time. Her smile was genuine when she left the church, and the familiar the weight on her chest had lifted. The healing process had just begun, but Chelsea knew that she would continue to come to the meetings and finish the class. Feeling lighter than she had in months, Chelsea started her car and drove away, tears dampening her stash of tissues once more. This time they were tears of thanksgiving. She knew the consequences of her abortion would never go away. She had lost a part of her family's legacy. She also knew that God had a way of giving beauty for the ashes His children created in their own lives. She had just experienced a small measure of His promise for the oil of joy for those who mourn.

Chapter Seventeen

Chelsea tendered her resignation at Gleason Pharmaceuticals and used some of her severance pay as a down payment on the little cottage just off of Main Street. Grandpa had offered to drive her to St. Louis to move her things home, but she had already engaged a moving company. It took her three days to pack, clean out her desk and say goodbye to her friends in St. Louis. As she set out for the long drive back to Purchase, she could only thank God for his mercy. The past was truly behind, and she was ready to start anew.

Gramps had looked a little sad as the movers unloaded her things in her new cottage, but Chelsea had gone back to her grandparents for a quick dinner. She was tired but happy by the end of moving day and ready to collapse in her old bedroom one last time. Gram had fixed meatloaf, mashed potatoes and home-grown green beans from the garden. They sat around the table and talked about grain prices, the weather and the job she had just taken at the Purchase Daily News.

As the ladies cleared the table, Grandpa walked over and eased himself down into his favorite chair. He bent over to look at Chelsea's portfolio that lay open on the coffee table.

"Looks like one of those coffee table books," he said, turning the pages one by one.

A flash of inspiration filled Chelsea and she saw a large flat book filled with the pictures she had taken since she'd been back home in Purchase. She could even imagine the gold, embossed letters on the cover that spelled out the title . . . *Going Home*. A chill ran through Chelsea's body as a dream began to take shape and then dimmed as doubts assailed her. Who was she to publish a book? She had made so many mistakes in her life. How could she think God would use her to do something like that?

She shook both the dream and the doubts from her mind and went to help Gram in the kitchen. She found her grandmother covered with flour from the waist and elbows down. Home-made noodles laid out on floured cheesecloth covered the countertop.

"Special occasion?" Chelsea asked, gently brushing flour off the older woman's cheek. She rested her head on her shoulder, absorbing the love, relishing these moments that had been so few and far between.

"We're having company tonight," Gram said, patting Chelsea's hand and resuming her task of cutting the last sheet of dough into flour covered strips. "Pops and Dane Ross are coming over."

"Stop, Gram," Chelsea said, taking a step back. "I don't need a boyfriend, and you don't need to be butting in. Besides, Dane already has a girl friend."

Gram gave Chelsea a steady look and leaned against the flour covered counter. "Chelsea, this has nothing to do with you and Dane. It has to do with Pops being stuck in his house for six weeks now. I thought it was time for him to start getting out. And where did you get the idea that Dane Ross had a girlfriend?"

Chelsea's face flushed as she backed away. She'd over-reacted again. She was looking forward to the next post abortion group meeting. She needed answers, and knew that God was using these women to help her find answers. She apologized to Gram for over-reacting and went upstairs to change. She wasn't in the mood to see anyone, especially Dane Ross. She'd have Gram make her excuses.

She was confused about her feelings for Dane. More than once she had wanted to pick up the phone and talk to him about her day. They had become good friends in the six weeks she had been home, but she knew he wanted nothing more than that. Connie had told her that she had never seen Lisa with Dane before that night in the ice cream shop, but Chelsea wasn't the type to horn in on someone else's relationship. She had plenty of things to keep her mind occupied, even if her heart was traitorous and wanted to see him. By the time the Ross's got here tonight, she'd be long gone.

Chapter Eighteen

Dane was looking forward to taking Pops to the Livingston's for dinner. He older man hadn't been cleared to drive yet, and although he'd been taking short trips around the farm in the pickup, he wasn't ready for the highway yet. Besides, he needed an excuse to see Chelsea.

Dane finished shaving and put on khakis and a light blue short sleeved dress shirt. He had to admit, he was always hungry for a home-cooked meal, but he was really looking forward to seeing Chelsea. He picked up his hat and a carefully wrapped package and went to find Pops. The package was part of the reason he wanted to see Chelsea. He grabbed his keys and walked his father to the truck. Closing the truck door behind Pops, he crossed over and hopped in behind the wheel. As he started the truck, he wondered how this last visit with Chelsea would end.

Pops took one look at Dane slid down in the seat and pulled his hat down over his eyes. Dane wondered if the pain was getting to him, but he realized there was a smile tugging at the corner of the older man's mouth. It looked suspiciously like a smirk.

What is he up to? Dane wondered. Seeing that the joke seemed to be private, Dane backed out of the barn and headed toward Chelsea's house. When had it become Chelsea's house? Butterflies lit and bounced in his stomach and he realized he was nervous.

Taking a deep breath, he let it out slowly. "Let's go have some fun, Pops." Dane said, looking over at his father.

"Somebody sure smells good," said a voice partially muffled by a hat.

Dane felt the heat rise in his face. He took his hat off and laid it on the carefully wrapped package on the seat between them. "You planning on meddling in my business all night?"

"Might be," was the only reply that came from under the hat. "Maybe somebody ought to before you lose that girl for good."

Dane shook his head at the old man's persistence, but refused to be baited into a discussion of his love life. Or lack of one. His father rarely gave him advice, and Dane gave more than passing thought to what his father had said. As the men drove the last few miles to the Livingston place, Dane realized that he might be running out of time.

Chelsea grabbed her sweater and her camera and left the house. It was six o'clock, and she wanted to be well out of the house before the Ross's arrived at six-thirty. She sat down on the back porch and tightened the laces of her hiking boots, then headed down the path through the back pasture to the Renault farm.

As she walked, she thought about all that had happened in the last six weeks. She knew she would receive the help she needed at the next few meetings of the post abortion group. She had reconnected with the tapestry of family and friends she had left behind, and made new ones. She felt her passion for her new career grow in leaps and bounds. She was happiest behind the camera. She had already designed business cards, and Marsha was helping her build a website. It seemed like her life was back on track. God had led her home, in more ways than one.

She had been saving some of her best photos and building her portfolio. At night she had been sitting down and writing stories to go with the pictures. Her book was taking shape in her mind. She had taken hundreds of pictures in the last few weeks, some of them stood out as stories in their own. Stories of life in a small town, a life that Chelsea had taken for granted.

Chelsea strolled through the perfectly formed lines of trees. By fall the acreage around her would be awash with brilliant color. She looked up as the maples shifted in the wind, flashing first green, and then silver as their leaves fluttered in the breeze. The tough smooth leaves of the oak trees spread like a canopy, waiting to shelter whatever sought refuge there. The birches were next, their white bark forming luminous lines in the sea of greens. Chelsea took several photos, adjusting the focus and light settings on the new camera she had bought with some of her severance pay. It would serve her well whether she was doing outdoor weddings or portraits in her studio. She walked along the rows of fruit trees that could trace their roots back to before Columbus had landed in the New World. She felt her roots go down too. With each step toward opening her new studio and her own restoration, she could feel a deep contentedness sink into her heart. She recognized it then. It was peace. Not because she had left the city, and not because she'd had the wrong job, but because she had come home in her heart.

She looked up to see she had wandered all the way to the pond near the back of the Renault's property. From where she was standing, she caught a glimpse of someone sitting on the log bench by the water's edge. It looked like someone was having some private time and Chelsea didn't want to interrupt. She started to back away, but from where she stood, she could see the man's chest heaving. She took two steps closer, wondering if he was in trouble. Was he crying? Was he hurt? Chelsea was torn between giving him privacy and seeing if he was alright. She took a few more steps forward, through the last of the trees, and the whole man came into view. Dane. Chelsea didn't know whether to be happy or mad. He was supposed to be at dinner at Gram's.

She made her way through the tall grass to where he sat and noticed that he seemed to be out of breath. "What are you doing here?" she asked.

He crossed his legs and looked up at her. "I was hoping to appear nonchalant," he said, giving her a broad grin. There was perspiration on his forehead and his breathing was still labored. "You got here too soon," he said. When Gramps had said she had come this way, Dane wasn't about to lose his last chance to talk to her before she left for the city. He had run the entire way. He had some things he needed to say to her. Things she might not be ready for, but he needed to say them. His heart stopped as she moved close enough that he could see that she was quivering. He'd wanted to take her in his arms for weeks now, to hold her against his heart and tell her everything would be alright. That he'd make it alright. Somehow. Now she stood before him, waiting. At once he knew that she was willing. He gently pulled her toward him, and felt her fit right into a place in his heart. He held her, wondering again at the trust she was placing in him. After he had done so badly and misunderstood so much, she was giving him another chance.

Chelsea shook with the effort it took not to totally yield into his embrace. She knew that once she did, she would never be the same again. She realized that he loved her, but there was still too much between them. She took a slow step back from his embrace and led him back to the bench.

She sat for a moment, and tried to gather her courage. She wondered if this would be a beautiful new beginning or the end of a good thing. She shifted to face him, but couldn't look in his eyes. "I did something, Dane, and I need to tell you about it."

Suddenly, the light came on, and understanding came. She wasn't haunted by the rape, it was something else, and as a youth pastor, he had seen the symptoms many times. How had he missed them with Chelsea? His mind began to count the weeks since the jury trial and her arrival in Purchase. Understanding dawned like a world that had rotated from darkness to light. The pain in her eyes hadn't been only for herself, but for the baby she no longer carried.

He understood how the abortion industry worked. Two young women at the campus ministry had told him about their experiences. They both had said that if they had known all the facts, their choices would have been different. He had watched them grieve and had done what he could to help them heal. So many young women having procedures that alter the rest of their lives.

All at once, Chelsea knew he knew. She resigned herself to her fate and decided to trust God no matter what happened. She looked up into his eyes, to see if her future would include the man she loved. Despite her best efforts at guarding her heart, she was in love with Dane Ross. And no matter what this moment cost her, she would never be sorry that she told him. She wanted a relationship with someone where there were no secrets.

Dane watched as the wall in Chelsea's eyes that had separated them came down and a look of determined resignation replaced it. He refused to let go of her hand as he let the new information settle in. He should have thought about it before. As they sat side by side, Dane let the words that were in his heart spill out. He knew his next words would make or break their relationship. "Chelsea, nothing you have done will make me care for you any less. He let those words sink in, and then went on. "Something terrible happened to you, and then something worse happened. Am I right?"

Chelsea nodded slowly and felt the air rush out of her lungs and the band that constricted her heart, that constrained every conversation and kept friends and family at a distance, loosen. Maybe this was part of God's plan. Maybe it was safe to trust this man. Taking a deep breath, Chelsea let out her secret. "I had an abortion, Dane. About eight weeks ago."

Dane started to take her in his arms, but Chelsea moved back, wanting to see his face. The look in his eyes told her all she really needed to know. She was accepted, not rejected. Loved and not despised. She felt the burden of shame lift from her shoulders as the look of love on Dane's face reminded her again that she wasn't alone, wasn't forsaken. She knew that she would never really be alone. She would always be her Heavenly Father's daughter, worthy of receiving all the benefits of being related to the King.

She knew that in the next few months of her life, there would be a series of these conversations. She needed to tell the people she loved, the people who had been affected by her abortion. She was sure that all the conversations wouldn't be this easy, but it was a beginning

Dane broke their embrace first and bent to pick up the package he had brought with him and handed it to Chelsea. With an unspoken question in her eyes, she took the square, flat package and began to unwrap it. She drew in a sharp breath. It was her butterfly picture. She had thought she would never see it again after that day at the Harvest of Talents. She gently rubbed her finger over the golden butterfly. She saw a picture of herself when she had first come home to Purchase. She had been poised on the tip of the flower, holding on tightly, balanced on her Father's love, afraid to spread her wings, afraid of falling.

Overwhelmed by what God had done in her life is such a short time, she sent up a silent prayer, thanking Him for the changes He had made in her heart. Then she turned her attention to the man sitting on the log beside her. "I don't know how to thank you for rescuing my picture," she said, lifting her eyes to look at the man she knew in her heart was the one for her.

"I wasn't sure what it meant to you, but I knew from your reaction, that it must have been important." He paused for a moment and took both of her hands in his. "I got everything wrong, these past few weeks, Chelsea. In my misguided effort to help, I managed to trample on all of your emotions. I'm sorry."

"I appreciated what you were trying to do. I saw your pastor's heart in your desire to help one of your sheep. That's not a bad thing," feeling the warmth of his fingers entwined with hers.

"That's what I thought it was at first too, Chelsea, but to be honest, I think I've loved you from the first time I saw you that day at the farm. I kept telling myself my interest was purely from a counselor's standpoint, but I've felt the connection to you and that photo since then."

Chelsea looked at the photo and back at Dane. What had he seen in the photo?

"I saw a butterfly. One I had hoped to help heal. I see now that God had a much bigger plan for both of us. I love you Chelsea, I don't want you leave. I know you're not ready now, but there's something I want to ask you." Dane got down on one knee in front of Chelsea as she sat on the log. "Would you marry me, Chelsea," he asked. "I'm willing to wait as long as you need."

Chelsea closed her eyes, overwhelmed by the goodness of God and the love of the man in front of her. She smiled at the kind, considerate man who was willing to walk through this journey of healing with her and nodded. They sealed her promise with a kiss, and Chelsea felt a new pathway of her destiny unfolding before her.

She held the picture up again in the soft evening light. She looked again at the butterfly and saw something completely different this time. She saw a golden butterfly surrounded by friends and family, standing on the tip of her destiny. Free to fly.

Epilogue

Chelsea walked down the aisle of the Purchase Community Church to the man she loved, her grandfather at her side, giving her away. Of course she wasn't going far. Her photography business was booming and her coffee table book was being published soon. Her book was dedicated to those, who like herself, had suffered the trauma of abortion and to those who were determined to share with them the message of God's love. She could feel God at work in her heart again, planting seeds of a new dream. She wanted to open a post abortion healing group at the Purchase Community Church. She wanted every hurting woman to know that she could go home.

If you've never met the Savior...

The most important thing I ever did in my life was ask Jesus into my heart. He is the answer to all of my questions, he is the 'fix' to all of my problems. I will never be alone again, because He lives in me. I don't know what I ever did without Him. He paid the price for all of my sins. They are washed away, and He remembers them no more...

If you don't know this amazing Savior, you can pray this prayer, or just pour out your heart to your Heavenly Father. He hears you when you pray.

Father, thank you that you loved me enough to send your Son to pay the price for all my sins, the big ones and the little ones. Thank you that as I ask you to forgive me, you are wiping my sins away with a heavenly eraser, never to be a weight in my life again. I give you my life, and I ask you to make me a child of the King, with all its blessing and privileges. I thank you that your plan for me is good, and I ask that you begin to reveal it to me now. Forgive me for where I've walked out of your path, and direct my feet back to your perfect will. I love you Lord. Thank you for saving me!

And now I will give you some advice I was given when I was first born again! Find a Bible believing church and plant yourself. Let your roots go down deep. Read the Bible every day. Talk to your Heavenly Father all the time! That's how relationships grow, by spending time together.

And now you, like Chelsea can say . . .

Scarcely had I passed by them, When I found the one I love . . .
Song of Solomon 3:4

Dedication

This book is dedicated to the women and men who work on the front lines of the fight against abortion. You are my heroes. Your voice is making a difference in the lives of thousands of women across the country. Thank you for laying down your lives to prevent stories like this one. A portion of the proceeds of this book will be donated to support their work.

And to the One who knows the secrets of our inward parts and loves us still . . .

If you would like more information, please e-mail Savannah at MyHeartHisHome2@gmail.com.

For reasons of confidentiality, we will not contact you unless you request a reply. If you would like to be on our mailing list so we can notify you of coming events, please indicate the address you'd like us to use in your e-mail.

Additional copies of this book may be purchased at the WestBow Press online bookstore at www.bookstore.westbowpress.com

Printed in the United States
By Bookmasters